home run

ALSO BY PAUL KROPP

For Parents
I'll Be the Parent, You Be the Kid
How to Make Your Child a Reader for Life
The Reading Solution

For Teens
Running the Bases
The Countess and Me
Moodkid and Prometheus
Moodkid and Liberty
Ellen, Eléna, Luna

For Younger Readers
Against All Odds
Avalanche
Hitting the Road
My Broken Family
Street Scene
What a Story!

home run

Paul Kropp

DOUBLEDAY CANADA

Library and Archives Canada Cataloguing in Publication

Kropp, Paul, 1948–
Home run / Paul Kropp.

ISBN-13: 978-0-385-66148-5
ISBN-10: 0-385-66148-7

I. Title

PS8571.R772H64 2006 jC813'.54 C2006-903185-1

Cover image: Rubberball/Getty Images
Cover and text design: Leah Springate
Printed and bound in Canada

Published in Canada by
Doubleday Canada, a division of
Random House of Canada Limited

Visit Random House of Canada Limited's website: www.randomhouse.ca

TRANS 10 9 8 7 6 5 4 3 2 1

Contents

1 A Father-Son Moment 1
2 Pledges 9
3 The Pyjama Party 15
4 Butter 21
5 Sweet Words and Sour 27
6 Prayers 35
7 The Grind 41
8 Gloriana 49
9 Trick and Treat 55
10 Counting to Three 63
11 Dysfunctional Thoughts 73
12 Nobody Messes With Pug 79
13 One Problem Resolved 87
14 The Most Frustrating Christmas Pageant Ever 93
15 True Love Doesn't Always Wait 101
16 Happy Holidays 107
17 The Great Unfolding of the World 113
18 Two Blasts of Heat 121
19 A Brief Cultural Excursion 127
20 So Much for Culture 133
21 Lineup 141
22 New Vows 151
23 The Muses 159
24 Farewell and Welcome 165
25 Slammed 173
26 At Last 187
27 Poet Laureate 191

Acknowledgements 195

vocab:

* admonititions!

- university freshman.

- trip out west - 3 days (driving to university)

* "slezy motels"

- intrests are:

- yellow card

- U2

& new fave group [Tinkertoys]

1

A Father-Son Moment

WITH ANY REASONABLE LUCK, I might have begun my university years by flying out west, unpacking a suitcase of clothes, setting up my computer, and waiting patiently while Greyhound shipped a few boxes of essential gear. But no. Somewhere in the how-to-be-a-parent guidebook it says that parents must *drive* their children to the school, transport the offspring and his/her goods to the dorm room, and then engage in tearful farewells and worthy admonitions.

Admonitions! Pretty good word, isn't it? See what being in first year has already done for me?

The trip out west took two days, and involved four stops for gas, five bathroom breaks, three fast-food meals, and one overnight stay in a sleazy motel. I was okay with the four stops, five breaks, and three quick meals. It was the overnight that was gruelling.

During the days, I was able to cocoon myself in the back seat of our old Ford, listening to various MP3s through my headphones. It was actually a fairly pleasant zone to be in, watching the landscape roll by, listening to Yellowcard and U2 and my new favourite group, the Thinkertoys.

I was interrupted only occasionally by my parents. My mom would turn back, shake my knee to get my attention, and then wait until I took off my headphones. "This is the Continental Divide," she would say.

I would respond "Oh," and put my headphones back on.

My mother and my father would return to their CDs of 1970s favourites and I would go back to the Thinkertoys. Cross-country trips do not make for parent-child bonding any more.

But our one overnight was difficult, at least for me. We had reached somewhere in Alberta—not Calgary, since that would have been too interesting—but some place where the only scenery was oil derricks. To save money, my father had booked a motel that looked like something out of *Psycho*. An Anthony Perkins look-alike was at the front desk, smiling politely. He gave my dad a key to our collective room: two queen beds, two bathroom towels, and plastic glasses wrapped in crinkly plastic wrappers. The only word to describe this level of elegance would be . . . sanitary. Even the toilet was covered with a piece of paper "for your protection," making you wonder what the toilet might do if it were not sealed up.

We had supper at the motel "restaurant." The quotation marks reflect the neon sign and the quality of food and service. It was the kind of place that made Harvey's seem like a big step up. The "restaurant" had hamburgers the consistency of leather anointed with ketchup that had a vague petroleum taste, as if it were diluted with something from the oil derricks in the distance. Still, the portions were big and the lemon-cream pie almost good, especially in comparison to everything else.

When we got back to the room, my parents put on the TV for *Law and Order* and I put on my headphones. I had brought a book for the trip, *The Iliad*, which I was trying to read in preparation for my Humanities class. I was not doing well with *The Iliad*, though my eyes kept going over the words. Maybe it's a book that you have to read without listening to the Thinkertoys at the same time.

Eventually I gave up and fell into a comatose state on the bed. There's another good word—deriving from *coma* (to which I was headed) and maybe *toes* (which were glad to be out of my shoes). I fell back on my bed and began thinking about sex.

I apologize for this. I realize that an eighteen-year-old guy about to enter university should be thinking about his studies, his future, his course reading lists, if not the deep meaning of *The Iliad*—whose surface meaning still escaped me. But I was not thinking about these things. I was thinking about Maggie, this red-headed girl I'd gone out with for the past year. I was thinking about her hair and her eyes, and the funny little laugh she has. Then I began thinking about how she always pushed my hands away when she decided that our making out had gone far enough.

Maggie and I had never had sex. That was pretty frustrating at the time, but probably for the best. At least, Maggie said it was for the best, and Maggie was smarter than me and right about so many things. At some level, Maggie knew she was destined for prime time, starting with heading east to the prestigious Sarah Lawrence College in New York state, while I was destined for afternoon soaps, and was headed west to the undistinguished Burrard University in Vancouver.

Prime-time people don't have sex with soaps people, it's as simple as that. Anyhow, I lay on the motel bed and began thinking how much I missed Maggie, even though we had never had sex. And soon I began thinking about *why* we never had sex, and then thinking about what sex would have been like if we had had it. The last thought was the most interesting, and I pursued that until I fell asleep.

I woke up about midnight when I heard a sound. In a flash, I became convinced that the Anthony Perkins look-alike in the lobby was now lurking in the room, or in the shower, or just over my bed . . . with a knife. Then, of course, I really woke up. But there was nothing to see in the dark room, and nothing more to hear until my mother whispered something like, "Go to sleep, dear."

But then I was wide awake, thinking about Maggie again. I remembered watching *Pyscho* as part of Maggie's Friday film society. I remembered how scared we got, and how much fun we used to have. Then I wondered how her frosh week would go at Sarah Lawrence. I wondered if she was happy, or if she missed me. Of course Maggie had moved on, and I was moving on, and then I felt sad about all that and fell back asleep.

The next day, we arrived at my BU dorm about three in the afternoon. The place was a hive of parents and kids, minivans and suitcases, confused expressions and looks of stern determination. The lucky students, the ones with smiles on their faces, lived close by.

Their parents had packed up their belongings, driven an hour or so, and then dropped off their son or daughter who had already arranged a dorm room with some high school friend. These kids were already paired up with one or two or a half-dozen people they knew.

Then there were the rest of us. Confused, awed, scared—if not quite willing to admit it. I had spent some time hanging around the local college back at home, so it wasn't so bad for me. But I could see other kids going around slack-jawed and stunned, overwhelmed by the size and anonymity of the place. It's a long way from high school in Podunk, Manitoba to the dorms at BU, and I'm not just speaking physical distance.

My dad helped me lug my belongings up to the dorm room. These were minimal: two suitcases of clothes, one computer and its assorted stuff, a box of my parents' suggested goodies like an alarm clock, a desk light and an iron (!), a backpack of *my* essential goodies like my CDs, my iPod, and a ratty toy hamster I'd had since the age of two. There were also a few books: three fantasy novels, *The Iliad* and *The Odyssey* (both second-hand), a book by somebody named Borges that Maggie had given me, and a book of selected poems of Shelley and Keats. These would suggest my impressive literary background to any girl I might be lucky enough to have visit my dorm room, providing I hid the three copies of *Maxim* magazine that I had also brought with me.

"Not bad," my father said when we reached the room. It was up three flights of stairs, so we were all out of breath.

"Not bad at all," I echoed.

That was a lie. My dorm room was only slightly larger than my bedroom at home, and it had to accommodate both me and some unknown roommate assigned by the university housing office. The room looked like it had been divided down the middle, with a single bed and a dresser-desk-closet combination on each side of the divide. At the end was a window, with a view of a parking lot. From the look of the left side of the dorm room, my roommate had already arrived. He had taken the sunnier side of the room, plopped down two suitcases and a couple boxes of books, and disappeared.

So I began putting my earthly possessions on the left side of the room, wondering what kind of roommate would actually leave a Bible on his bed.

"The room's not very large," my mother said. She's a master of understatement.

"It's the best we could do," my father grumbled. In truth, I was on a "Macklin family scholarship"—my parents were paying—so I ended up with the cheapest dorm room and the cheapest meal plan. I figured my roommate was in the same financial boat, floating just over the poverty waterline.

"But it *is* clean," my mother replied brightly. "So don't go making a mess, Alan." I think this comment was meant to be encouraging.

One more trudge up and down the stairs and all my gear had made it to the bedroom. I was now officially installed as a student at Burrard University—probably the least famous school in Vancouver.

"Now where would the bathroom be?" my mother asked.

"Maybe down the hall," I told her.

"Then I'm going to freshen up," she said.

"They're coed," I called after her, but my words didn't quite reach her in time.

That left my father and me, alone together and feeling awkward, as we always did in such situations. I'm not sure if he's more awkward with me than I am with him, but it doesn't matter much since the *general* awkwardness ends up quite high regardless. After a moment of silence, my father cleared his throat and looked at me.

"Well, Alan, I guess this is it," he said. Since this remark had no meaning, I took it as a verbal throat-clearing.

"Guess so," I replied.

"We won't see you until Thanksgiving, or maybe Christmas," he said.

"Guess not."

He paused, looked out the window at my sort-of view, then turned back in my direction. "I suppose you know how, uh, important this is. I mean, you're the first person in our family to actually attend university, and your mother and I are very proud, you know."

I believe I was blushing. I believe my father was blushing. It wasn't clear who was more embarrassed by this little speech.

"Anyhow, I wish I had some great words of wisdom to encourage you as you start off, but I don't." He stopped, looked at the floor and then at my mattress. "We hope you do well and, uh, don't make foolish mistakes."

"I won't, Dad," I said.

"But just to be on the safe side," he said, clearing his throat again, "I bought you these."

My father reached into his gym bag and brought out a box—a box of a dozen condoms.

"Dad," said, "I still haven't used the first one you gave me."

My father shook his head. "You don't have to lie to me, Alan. I know what I was like at your age and, well, I just want you to be a little more careful." He handed me the box. "Now get these out of sight before your mother comes back. I don't want her to think I'm encouraging you. And I am *not* encouraging you, understand?"

"Got it," I told him. "You just want me to be careful."

"As Yogi Berra once said, 'Don't screw up.'"

"Did he really say that?"

"Something like that," my dad muttered, just as my mother came rushing back into the dorm room.

"Did you know those bathrooms are *coed*?" my mother demanded, as if this were the strangest thing in the world. "A boy came in and sat down in the stall right beside me."

"That's how a coed bathroom works, Mom," I said.

"Well, it was disgusting! Alan—whatever you do—respect other people's privacy."

My second bit of advice for the afternoon. "I will, Mom."

She seemed relieved. My dad decided it was time for the two of them to make their exit.

"Good luck, Alan," my dad said. He reached out to shake my hand, which I took as a sign of my new maturity.

"And you call every other night," my mother said, a bit teary-eyed either from the situation here or the distress in the bathroom. "As soon as you get a phone, you call."

"Yes, Mom," I said as she kissed both cheeks and my lips.

"Be careful with your money, Al," my father added. Now the advice was coming fast and loose. "The dime you save today is a dollar you can spend tomorrow."

"Don't get in trouble," my mother said as she went down the hall. And then the two of them disappeared down the stairs.

I breathed a sigh of relief and went back into the dorm room. I pulled out the box of condoms my father had given me. They were genuine Trojans, but only average size. I didn't know if I should feel insulted.

I was holding the box of condoms in my hand when a face appeared at the doorway. It was quite a handsome face, really, with dark eyes, a straight nose with flared nostrils, and a chiselled jaw. The face reminded me of half a dozen Hollywood actors, from Hugh Grant to Brad Pitt, without specifically looking like any one of them.

"Hi, there, I'm Kirk." He put out his hand.

I had to move the condom box from my right hand to my left to shake.

"I'm Alan. Alan Macklin."

"We're roommates," he went on, as if this were especially good news. "I guess you just got in."

"Yeah," I replied. "Just made it through all the worthy admonitions and the tearful farewells," I said.

"You must be an English major," he said. "I'm in theology."

"You mean, like, God?"

"I mean, like, religion."

This was something of a conversation stopper. Suddenly I was embarrassed about even holding the box of condoms. We both seemed to be staring at the box.

"Well, uh, this was a kind of parting gift from my dad," I explained. "Enough for the next four years at the rate I'm going. I mean, if you ever run short, just let me know."

He was still smiling like the televangelists you see on VisionTV. "I wouldn't need one of those," he said.

I gave him a look. Since I barely knew him, this wasn't the time to ask the obvious question. Nonetheless, he gave me an answer.

"You see," Kirk explained, "I've taken the pledge."

2

Pledges

AT THE END of that first day, I did what any self-respecting person does after a difficult time: I sat down at my computer and sent emails. In the old days, at home, I'd just IM people because our lives seemed like they were all connected. Now I was way out west, so we were down to email—in touch but more remote.

The person I emailed first was Maggie, former girlfriend, former dating advisor, current subject of too many late-night dreams, and probably my best friend.

From: amacklin@BU.edu
To: maggiemac@sl.edu
Moving in has been gruelling. My roommate is a born-again something, my mother thinks this place is disgusting, and my father thinks I'm a sex maniac. It's enough to make me feel nostalgic for high school. Only bright spot on the horizon is that my parents are gone and have left me in peace. Please tell me not to jump off a bridge.

From: maggiemac@sl.edu
To: amacklin@BU.edu
Don't jump off a bridge by yourself. But if you find a good one let me know and I'll join you. I feel like the proverbial fish out of water here: I don't have the right clothes, the right attitudes, or the right pedigree. My roommate has such a dizzying social life that I've only

seen her for twenty minutes since arrival, and that was twenty minutes with her looking down her nose at me. This borders on excruciating.

I spent the rest of the evening emailing my other good friends—Scrooge and Jeremy—and then my second-string friends, all of them spread over the country at various colleges and universities, all of them feeling vaguely lost and confused judging from the emails I got back.

My life became more complicated the next day when Kirk decided to join the ranks of my friends. It's very difficult, when someone decides to become your friend, to say "no, thanks"—especially when the prospective friend is very polite.

The next morning began with a cheerful wake-up suggestion from my roommate, "Hey, Al, let's have breakfast." I groaned and went back to sleep. That afternoon, when we met our dorm counsellors, it was Kirk who plopped down beside me and listened cheerfully while we were warned about the evils of drinking, drugs, sex, and failure to keep up with the course work. And it was Kirk who said, afterwards, "Let's get dinner over at Slavin." I had no reason to refuse.

So we stood in line at Slavin Hall—alias The Slop House or Sloppy Joe's—waiting for the elderly cafeteria ladies to put some appropriate slop on our trays. Tonight's dinner consisted of roast-beef slop, mashed-potato slop, and something that looked like carrot-and-turnip slop, all looking like they had been shaped with an ice cream scoop.

"I love this kind of food," Kirk said as we moved along the line.

"You do?"

"Sure. It's great down-home cooking, just like the ladies' group makes for our church. What's not to like?"

"The flavour," I said, "or lack of it."

"Al, I think you've got to perk up," he said, looking quickly in my direction as he took a second slice of apple-slop pie. "School can be a wonderful experience if you just learn to embrace it."

Kirk actually spoke like that, a mixture of high school guidance counsellor-speak with enthusiastic phrases that you might see on a poster in a dentist's office. I thought, at the time, that Kirk might really see life like that, but things turned out not to be so simple.

We sat down with a bunch of other first-year students to the right of the entrance. Somehow, second- and third-year students found a way to avoid dining in Slavin even if they were on a meal plan, but first-years clustered together like the pathetic little souls they—I should say "we"—happen to be.

"So, Al," my roommate began, "tell me about yourself."

For a fleeting moment, I was tempted to feign illness and escape, but then I remembered that he was my roommate, and that I was stuck with him for at least a semester.

"Hmmm," I began instead. "How about white, non-smoker, sometimes-drinker, occasional thinker. That kind of sums it up."

"Hey, that's good," he said, flashing those pearly teeth. "You're funny. That was the first thing I noticed about you. I wrote a letter to my family last night and said that I had a really funny roommate."

"Funny ha-ha, I hope. Not funny weird."

A perplexed look came over his face. It was as if he had to translate what I had just said into his own language before he could get it. Then he laughed, not a lot, but enough. "See, you *are* funny."

"And you?" I asked. My mouth was full of congealed gravy, potatoes, and mushy roast beef, so I couldn't say much more.

"In high school, they used to say I was a pretty serious guy," Kirk replied. "But I'm not sure about that. Some people think you're dull just because you don't want to shoot squirt guns at Bible camp."

"Right," I said, not because this made much sense, but because *Right* is a very good thing to say in almost any circumstance. It suggests (a) that I'm listening, (b) that I agree, and (c) that I want to hear more.

Kirk went on to tell me about the rest of his life: the wonderful family back home, his fabulous girlfriend, the ranch where he grew up, the small religious school he'd attended. It was a touching story, really, like an episode of *Little House on the Prairie*.

Kirk was the kind of person who gestured with his hands when he talked. This brought attention to his fingers, which were long, and to the ring on his left fourth finger. I had to stare hard, but then I could read the words: True Love Waits.

"Interesting ring," I said. "It almost asks a question, like, waits for what?"

Kirk smiled and didn't miss a beat. "Waits for marriage," he replied. "I got it after the pledge."

"The pledge?"

"The abstinence pledge," he went on. He said this with an absolutely straight face, as if it were the most normal thing in the world. "Everyone in my high school did the pledge, but I went a step further and got the ring."

"Abstinence meaning what?" I asked him. "Abstain from booze, drugs, sex?"

Kirk smiled. "We made a commitment to a life of purity." He looked at me when I frowned. "I mean, clean living. So we've got to abstain from all that. No corrupt images and no sex before marriage."

Once again I had to translate. No corrupt images = no porn; no sex before marriage = no sex for an eternity. Now I understood why Kirk had a computer without email or an Internet connection. He was simply cut off from the world of sin, a world I was so desperately trying to join.

"So can you, like, look?" I asked him. At that moment a particularly striking blonde was coming through the slop line and waiting at the cashier. "Can you look at a girl like that one over there, or would that be too much lust?"

"Oh, no, we can *look*," Kirk said, following my gaze. "We just can't touch."

"Right," I said, repeating myself. "You're saving yourself for marriage."

"That's the pledge," he replied. "It's a goal I've set for myself. Kathy and I both pledged that we would wait."

"Kathy?"

"My girlfriend. Almost my fiancée."

"*Almost* because you haven't asked her?"

"Right," Kirk replied. Now it was his turn to use the word. He did seem a bit embarrassed by this question, though. It was the first time I'd seen him look less than perfectly self-assured.

"But you're going to ask her."

"Right. As soon as I graduate, or maybe before," Kirk replied.

"Hmmm," I said. *Hmmm* is a cut up from *Right* on the response chart. *Hmmm* is the kind of thing a doctor says when you're describing the funny tumour growing on some private part of your body; *Right* is what guys say to acknowledge that something is correct, unless there's an extra letter i, as in *Ri-ight*, which mean that something is obviously not correct. Is it any wonder that English is so difficult to learn?

"So that's your goal, then, to abstain?" I asked.

"No, I want to get my degree and then go on to divinity school. I'm going to be a preacher," he said, pausing. "No, I'm going to be one of the great preachers."

"But why here? Why did you come to this wretched hive of scum and villainy?"

Kirk looked at me with a raised eyebrow. He must have been impressed by the vocabulary, so I didn't bother to tell him that the line was borrowed from *Star Wars*.

"So I can learn about the devil where he lives."

Talk about conversation stoppers! A guy who says he's come gunning for the devil and then looks you right in the eyes, well, it makes you begin to sweat just a little.

"And what about you, Al? Why are you here?"

I felt awkward, like some mashed potatoes had lodged in my throat. "I . . . uh . . . I'm kind of interested in Keats and Shelley. You know, poetry."

He was still looking at me. Kirk had very intense way of looking at you. Guys rarely look at each other directly, or even indirectly for more than a second or two, but Kirk just kept staring at me. Obviously he didn't believe a word that I said. This wasn't surprising, because I didn't either.

"Okay, that's just a line," I admitted. "Mostly I'm just interested in girls."

"What's that?"

"Uh, girls," I repeated. "Mostly, I think, I just want to get laid."

I got the shocked look I expected, and maybe deserved.

Back in high school, the getting-laid comment was quite true. That's what it's like when you're sixteen or seventeen. But now that I'm older, life has become more complex. I really do like Keats and Shelley, the handful of their poems that I've read, and I'm really not *only* interested in sex, but that doesn't mean I'm not horny half the time. This is normal, I think. Most of my friends have already had sex, or so they say, and that might make me the last remaining eighteen-year-old virgin on the planet, excluding Kirk, of course, who's prepared to wait for it. Maybe I should read the *Kinsey Report* and check, but I think eighteen year olds *should* be thinking about sex half the time. What's the alternative? Politics? Philosophy? Economics? The world is full of excruciatingly dull topics that I might want to think about when I'm older, like thirty or forty.

So our awkward dinner concluded and we began to walk out of the cafeteria. That's when I saw the Pajama Party flyer on the wall. It was all part of the Frosh Week hoopla, a five-day binge of sports, parties, meetings, and library tours. Note the incongruity. I suspected the sports and parties were there only to encourage us to take the library tour. But there was the poster: "Pajama Party Friday. Wear your best or your worst, but wear something! Come!"

I looked at Kirk, then at the poster, and I began to get the germ of an idea.

3

The Pajama Party

"WHY DO I HAVE to go with you?" Kirk whined.

"Because you're my roommate and that's what roommates do," I began. "And because you said you wanted to learn about the devil where he lives. Well, if the devil doesn't live at this pajama party, then I'll be very disappointed."

"Get Fuji to go," Kirk said. He was referring to a guy in the next dorm room who played strange music late at night.

"Fuji can't go anywhere without his computer. He may not even own pajamas."

The guy in the room next door was actually named Franklin but he was permanently tied to his Fujitsu laptop, hence the nickname.

"But *you're* not wearing pajamas," Kirk said at last.

I could tell he was crumbling. "These *are* my pajamas, or as close as I've got to pajamas," I explained. My outfit consisted of a pair of cotton shorts and a wrinkled T-shirt from an old Thinkertoys concert. I felt it communicated a certain sense of cool, without going overboard. "Besides," I went on, "you've got real pajamas and a robe, for God's sake." Then I realized my slip. "Oh, sorry."

"Forgiven," Kirk replied.

"So you'll come?" I was begging at this point, but what was a little lost pride compared to the prospect of going to this event on my own?

"Okay, but you'll owe me one," Kirk replied. He looked quickly into his closet for something to wear.

In his pajamas Kirk appeared, well, dapper. There's another excellent word that has dropped out of the language. In the old days, guys like Cary Grant were always dapper, but Brad Pitt? No, it's mostly a lost concept. We talked about that once at Maggie's Friday film society back home, the disappearance of dapper. Pretty impressive discussion that night. Anyhow, Kirk was wearing pajamas that looked like they'd been ironed and a bathrobe that was almost elegant. I half expected to see him smoking a pipe just to complete the look.

So dapper Kirk and rumpled me headed across the quad to Eggers Hall, the student centre. This was a stark, white building that must have been designed by a Japanese architect who had played too many years with Lego sets. Endowed by a rich man named Eggers, it was now referred to by many names: The Egg, Eggs and Ham, Eggo Hall, and, my own favourite, Egregious Hall. Remind me, when I die, never to endow a hall with the name Macklin.

We arrived fashionably late, as I planned, to enter a party in full non-swing. The problem with official university parties for first-year students is that most of us aren't officially old enough to drink. It is not that we *don't* drink, but that we're legally not supposed to drink. The Burrard U lawyers, in their wisdom, have pointed out the infraction of serving liquor to kids under nineteen, so all they offered was punch—like at a high school dance. The absence of alcohol for all these kids, many of whom began illicit drinking years ago at the ripe age of eight or twelve or thirteen, was sure to put a damper on events. At this pajama party, the girls were literally on one side of the room, the boys on the other (so reminiscent of first-year high school dances), and the DJ was playing entirely for his own amusement.

"I'm bored," I said.

"I'm amazed," Kirk replied.

Around us were maybe a hundred first-year students, all dressed in pajamas. The guys tended to favour outfits like mine, casual running shorts and cut-offs with T-shirts flopping over; the girls were in soft cotton pajamas, usually with robes to cover most of their sleeping outfits. The guys came as they often were, half-shaved, half-rumpled, half-dressed; the girls all wore makeup and had done something—whatever it is that girls do—with their hair.

"A den of iniquity," I said, using another *Star Wars* line. This was half-ironic, since there was no real iniquity in evidence: no revealing clothing, no suggestive behaviour, nothing lewd or the least bit lascivious.

"Really?" Kirk asked.

"I could only hope."

We went to the refreshment window to pick up two non-alcoholic punches, then turned back towards the crowd, pseudo-drinks in hand.

"This reminds me of church camp."

"Oh? You wore pajamas at church camp?" I asked.

"No, it's just that people are feeling awkward. They need to loosen up."

"You loosened up at church camp?"

"Of course we loosened up," Kirk snapped. "For one thing, we all danced. At least, that's where I learned how to dance. Would you hold my bathrobe?"

With one quick gesture, Kirk took off his silky Ralph Lauren-style robe, handed it to me, and walked across the room. I saw him looking at the tables of first-year girls until he picked one terrifically unlovely girl and stopped at her table. *What is he doing?* I asked myself. The answer was soon clear: he was inviting her to dance. In almost no time, the girl took off her robe and walked with Kirk to the dance floor.

The DJ, eyeballing two people who might actually get the party going, obliged with some music that had a beat. Kirk and the girl began to dance. Once again, I thought I was in a 1940s film. They were doing something—the waltz, the two-step, the marimba . . . what do I know about dances?—with a kind of effortless grace. They danced that number, then changed steps to a second song. By then, everyone in the room was watching them, or pretending not to watch them, or making fun of them, but otherwise giving them all the attention we had to give.

When that number was finished, three girls (three!) came up to Kirk, all begging to dance. Kirk picked one of them, the music began again, and a few other couples—mostly girls dancing with girls—got up on the floor. Somehow, without seeming to work very hard at it, Kirk had started the party.

We spent three hours at the pajama party, long enough for Kirk to have danced with virtually every girl in the room, including several who had obviously been born with two left or cloven feet. The atmosphere was contagious enough that I even did a little dancing myself.

I do the white-guy shuffle, as my black friend Scrooge calls it, a kind of talentless pushing and shoving of hands and feet in vague time with the music. Unlike the ballroom dancing that Kirk had mastered, my dancing is strong on "cool" and weak on movement. It seemed good enough in high school, but with Kirk sweeping around the floor doing dance after dance, my own effort seemed a bit flimsy.

It was sufficient, though, to get a smile from a girl named Shauna who lived over in Houser House (nicknamed House House, Hoser House, Bowser House, Who's House Is This Anyway House, etc.). She was a blonde girl, with a light dusting of freckles and lovely pale blue eyes under thin, pale eyebrows. I immediately decided that she was the most beautiful girl I've ever seen, but I've made this judgment several dozen times in the past. Shauna and I danced a little, then I stopped at her table to talk, and finally she gave me her cell number with a giggle and a smile.

"Quite the party," Kirk said as we headed back to our dorm.

"Did you see the devil?"

He shot me a look. "What makes you think that Christians can't have fun?"

"Not sure," I replied, a bit troubled. "I thought fun was a heathen thing."

"Wrong again, Al," he sighed. "Wrong again."

"So I got a phone number," I said, pulling out a scrap of paper with Shauna's cell scribbled on it. "How about you?"

"I'm not looking for a girlfriend. I've got one back home," he replied. This was the famous Kathy, a girl who sent a lovely perfumed letter to Kirk every day, and whose devotion was by now legendary, at least in our dorm.

"Yeah, right," I said. Maybe I should have added the extra *i*: *ri-ight*. "The girls were all over you tonight, so what did you get?"

"Lots of dancing," he replied.

"Yeah?" It was that leading-question yeah.

"And there's this girl who really likes ballroom dancing," Kirk added. "She wondered if I'd help her practise some steps."

"Steps?"

"Yeah, steps."

"Ri-ight," I responded.

4

Butter

From: amacklin@BU.edu
To: maggiemac@sl.edu
Went with roommate to a pajama party. He gets all the girls and does all the dancing, I get to stand around and hold his bathrobe. Is this fair? I mean, is this FAIR?

From: maggiemac@sl.edu
To: amacklin@BU.edu
Wish we had a pajama party here. There's a group getting ready to re-enact ancient Greek games, and another putting on an all-girl *Lysistrata*, and the girl down the hall wants to set up a Simone de Beauvoir reading group. Not only don't I have the right clothes; I don't have the right kind of brain. Missing you, my sweet numbskull.

Perhaps I was inspired by the numbskull reference, but on Friday night I was actually in my bed reading Keats. I'm not kidding. Me, Al Macklin, reading Keats. Now that doesn't mean I was understanding Keats, but the poetry was at least passing in front of my eyes when I heard Kirk come in from the bathroom.

"You ready?" he asked.

"What?" I shouted back.

"Didn't you get the note I left on your bed? We're going dancing."

I closed my book and looked up. "You and me are dancing?"

Kirk must have seen the look of alarm in my eyes. His voice became very calm. "No, we're going to a dance club with those girls from Houser that we met at the pajama party. Remember? I think that girl Shauna likes you. Anyhow, she called and said a bunch of them were going to Butter and they wanted us to go with them, so I figured you'd want to go."

"Butter?"

"It's a dance club, they say, off campus," Kirk explained. "And there's no way I'm going there alone with all those girls. It's too exhausting. Besides, I explained all this in the note."

"The missing note," I said. "Fuji must have snuck into the room and stolen it."

"Actually, Fuji is coming with us," Kirk told me.

"Fuji? Dancing?" The idea was just too incredible. And if even Fuji was going, how could I just stay back and sit around the dorm?

"The girls are waiting," Kirk insisted. "Put on your dancing shoes and off we go."

Of course I didn't have dancing shoes, but I did have a pair of deck shoes that would do the job. Kirk did have dancing shoes, kind of shiny ones with slippery soles that made dancing easier—or so he said. I also put on my one semi-cool outfit so that I fit in with the local club scene. At least I looked cooler than Kirk, who was dressed like he was going to a church youth group, kind of neat and squeaky clean. Some day I'll have to explain to Kirk that squeaky clean has been out of fashion for a good forty years, ever since the days of Cary Grant. Then again, Kirk was cooler than Fuji, who wore a brightly coloured T-shirt and wrinkly pants that made him look vaguely like a fire hydrant. He told us it was his DDR outfit, based on some kind of computer dance game.

The three of us went over to Houser to pick up Shauna and a large group of girls from her dorm—perhaps that would be a gaggle of girls. Certainly they were all giggling and gabbing like a gaggle of girls might do.

I had spoken to Shauna a couple of times that week, but there hadn't been much of a romantic buzz over the cell phone. She was cute, of course, but kind of giggly and kind of air-headed compared to someone like, well, Maggie. Then again, almost any girl is airheaded compared to Maggie, who even makes me feel pretty dumb at times.

Nonetheless, Shauna looked just excellent that evening. She was wearing a tight, shiny shirt and some extraordinarily tight jeans that made her look very, very hot. Even so, Shauna couldn't compare to the girl who had latched on to Kirk. That girl was a dark-eyed, dark-haired beauty named Rachel who had a wonderful air of mystery about her.

Kirk, of course, had paid no particular attention to her, even though she called him daily and actually got him over to their dorm one day to practise some ballroom dance steps. I believed Kirk's mind was actually on higher things; unlike my own mind, which was always trying to crawl its way up from the gutter.

So the gaggle of girls and the three of us got on the city bus and were deposited, twenty minutes later, outside a club called Butter. I wondered if there are people who specialize in coming up with club names. I mean, why Butter rather than Margarine or Extra Virgin Olive Oil? Perhaps these names are tested on focus groups, like TV ads, to see what they evoke.

The bunch of us slid into Butter (pardon the pun) thanks to a collection of fake and real IDs. Inside, we found that the DJ was playing a strange mix of dance music. There were obviously couples who took this whole ballroom dancing thing very seriously—guys who looked like Richard Gere, and actually dressed to fit the image; girls who looked like Jennifer Lopez and stayed close to their boyfriends/dance partners. Then there were the usual club hangers-on: the tables of guys in baseball jerseys with pitchers of beer, the tables of girls with too much makeup waiting desperately for some male attention while, at the same time, trying to pretend that they were absolutely indifferent to any of the single guys in the room, and the tables of friends who were just looking for a fun night out. I guess we fell into that last category.

Except for Shauna, who had an agenda.

"I'm so glad you came with us, Alan," she told me.

There are various ways to deliver a sentence like that. For some girls, it would be deep and sultry, with a big emphasis on the *so*. For other girls, like my friend Maggie, it would be a simple statement of fact, as in, I'd rather be here with you than here without any guy at all. But Shauna decided to punctuate her phrasing in a very physical way. She pushed the side of her body quite persistently into my arm.

"Well, I'm just glad to see you again." I put my emphasis on the word *you* and Shauna responded by rubbing up against me even more obviously. It was as if our bodies were having their own wordless conversation.

One of the other girls interrupted that conversation. "Alan, get over here. Kirk is going to teach you how to dance."

"He is?" I asked.

"He is," the girl said, emphatically, grabbing my arm to drag me away from Shauna.

Kirk was surrounded by a semicircle of girls when I was dragged before him. He looked somewhat apologetic.

"They thought I could show you a few moves," he said, nodding at the half-gaggle.

"Yeah," cried one of the girls. "No more white-man's shuffle."

Was I red in the face at this point? Fortunately the lights in the club were so dim that my skin tone would be hard to determine.

"Can't you get Fuji for this?" I snarled.

"Fuji dances just fine," Kirk replied. I looked over to see the human fire hydrant doing some kind of bizarre robotic dance, as if he were a pixilated character from a video game. Still, he was dancing with a girl and did seem quite confident in his moves—more than could be said for me.

"So, Al," Kirk began, "the key thing is this—you dance with your body, not with your feet. You've got to loosen up to dance. Now just try this."

Kirk did an artful little manoeuvre that seemed to wiggle his entire spine, one vertebra at a time, from his butt to his shoulders. The girls applauded.

"Now you try," he said. I believe he was attempting to be encouraging.

I tried to wiggle, twisting first my butt, and then my midriff, and then my shoulders. I must have looked like a robot doing the rumba. The girls giggled.

"Loose, Al, loose!" Kirk suggested. "Try it again."

This time Kirk put his hands on my waist, as if this laying-on-of-hands would somehow help me move more fluidly. Instead, the thought of how this would look to Shauna and the other girls turned me into a petrified stick of wood. I got worse. The girls hid their giggles, but I knew. I knew.

"Okay, just try shaking everything," Kirk suggested.

This I could do. But I have to note a significant difference here. When a dancer shakes, it has a kind of effortless quality that is both limp and controlled. It looks, although casual, kind of artsy. When I shake, I look like some poor guy with palsy.

It was Rachel who brought this torture to an end. "Al, not everyone's a natural-born dancer, but at least you gave it a shot." Then she turned to Kirk and gave him one of those sultry looks. "Let's go dance."

One of the other girls took my hand and led me onto the floor. She smiled politely, then began doing some kind of dance routine that I might have seen once in a film. Fortunately, she required no assistance on my part. I did my white-man's shuffle; she wiggled and dipped and cavorted around me.

Out of the corner of my eye, I could see Kirk and Rachel floating about the dance floor, looking like polished professionals right out of *Shall We Dance?* I half expected to see numbers pinned to their backs so the judges could give them a score: "And the prize for the two-step goes to couple number 43, Kirk and Rachel!"

It was this thought that led to my muscles going strangely awry. My feet continued to shuffle, but somehow my chest pointed one way and my arms waved the other and I lost my balance. I would have fallen to the floor, but Shauna came up and caught me from behind.

"May I cut in?" she said to the girl who had been dancing around me.

In a moment, Shauna was in front of me dancing a white-girl shuffle to the music. This fact alone made me think that Shauna was worthy of more attention. The more I looked, the more I realized that she was really quite attractive.

"I think I could use a drink," I told her when the song ended. Behind us, the remainder of the girls were begging Kirk for a dance while Fuji just kept on going as if he were powered by Energizer batteries.

"Me too," she said. And we headed over to the safety of the bar.

I ordered two beers for us and raised one to my lips. Our dancing had given us both a sheen of sweat, a glow that seemed very attractive in her case.

"Rachel's got the hots for your roomie," she said as our drinks arrived.

"Well, good luck to her. He's born-again, you know."

"And what about you?"

"I was barely born the first time," I said.

"I'm so glad you were," Shauna replied.

By now, she was very, very close to me. Our faces were barely inches apart. I was looking deeply into her eyes, feeling the heat of her as she pressed into my chest. I could have kissed her. I wanted to kiss her. But I remembered some of Maggie's advice, something about "Less is more," so I held back. It was Shauna who made the move.

"My roommate's gone home for the weekend," she said. "I've got the place to myself."

"Oh," I said. Suddenly my throat felt very dry.

"Why don't we go back and see if my plants need watering."

5

Sweet Words and Sour

"WHY DON'T WE go back and see if my plants need watering?" might be among the sweetest words ever uttered in our language. Unlike Mae West's old line—"Why don't you come up and see me some time?"—these words have some subtlety. They might even rival the famous words of Keats, if I could actually remember what some of those famous words were.

Regardless, I wasn't about to say no.

We managed to duck out of Butter without our exit being observed by either Kirk or the gaggle. For a passing moment, I felt a bit guilty for leaving Kirk on his own. I also felt a little regret over the waste of a ten-dollar cover charge. But the wonderful thing about raw lust is that it manages to overcome both guilt and regret in fairly short order.

Huddled together waiting for the bus, my nose pressed into Shauna's blonde hair, I realized that this might be the big one. Ultimate goal number one—end of virginity. Here was a lovely girl, pressing against me, smelling delightfully of some flowery perfume, obviously interested in me. If I just managed to avoid making mistakes, I might end up in the sack.

I mentally reviewed all those pieces of advice I'd been given by Maggie two years ago, back when she was my dating advisor and not my girlfriend: Don't push too fast, don't grab, don't fondle, don't stick your tongue down her throat. I think those were all the don'ts. Now what were the dos? Do look in her eyes, do touch her gently, do compliment her, do make her feel beautiful and smart and important. So many dos and don'ts to think about all at once.

The bus came and we gratefully climbed on board. The night had turned cool and the bus was pleasantly warm. We took a seat at the back and I kissed Shauna's hair. Then she looked up and we began a gentle kiss that turned into something a little more frantic. In fact, all this might have led to serious making-out on the bus, but some old guy muttered "Get a room," and that put a little damper on our growing attraction.

I pulled back and tried to think of something we could talk about for the remainder of the ride. The problem, of course, was that I hardly knew Shauna. We shared no classes, had only spoken a couple of times either in person or on the phone, and had yet to discover anything we had in common. It occurred to me that I didn't even know her last name.

I panicked. Was I finally going to score a home run with a girl I hardly knew? After all these years of chasing, dating, and lusting after dozens of girls whom I actually knew and even liked, was I going to have sex with a girl whose name I only half knew? How could I do something like that? Is sex something so significant, or maybe so insignificant, that I could throw away everything I thought about relationships just to get this girl into the sack? Was I that shallow?

Indeed, I was.

Was I ready? I hadn't brought a condom; I hadn't even been thinking about sex when the evening began. I was reading Keats, thinking about nineteenth-century British landscapes and the sublime—whatever that is—and now my whole being was focused on one thing. Maybe Shauna would have a condom; maybe she was on the pill; maybe I should use a condom even if she was on the pill. I had a quick flashback to those STD videos they showed us in high school. *No, not that, anything but that!*

But maybe I was getting carried away. Maybe Shauna just wanted to water her plants. Maybe she was a serious indoor gardener. Maybe she was growing some especially delicate orchid that required precise waterings at particular times. Maybe my fantasies were overtaking some simple and innocent realities.

All these thoughts, all these troubling questions, flashed through my brain as fast as the little synapses up there could fire. But there were other words playing through my mind at the same time, words that overpowered doubt and guilt and thought. *Go for it, Al. It's time.*

So we travelled across town, Shauna saying something and me responding that her words were brilliant or lustrous or fascinating. Maybe they were, but I was only half listening. The rest of my mind was going through the dos and don'ts, the fears and the desires. At last we reached the school.

"It's our stop," Shauna said.

More magical words.

I took her hand and walked with her across campus to Houser, cutting in through the side door and up three flights of stairs to her room. She unlocked the door and I stepped into a twin-bedded dorm room that Shauna obviously shared with another girl.

"Pretty sweet," I said, looking around the room.

How much could I learn about Shauna from her room, her defined space on campus? I studied the walls, the posters, the notes. Shauna's side of the room was clearly marked with a large letter S mounted over her bed. It was decorated in pinks and oranges, a colour scheme that went from the comforter on her bed to the mirror on the wall. There was a large IKEA bulletin board with cutout pictures and magazine snippets pinned on to it. She obviously had dozens of girlfriends, all of them with longish dark hair and a fondness for baseball caps. There were guys on the board as well, maybe brothers, maybe old boyfriends, and a few magazine models with bulging pecs and washboard abs.

The magazine snippets might reveal something if I could interpret them: Hot Leprechaun, Ooops, First Year!, Party!, Downtown Me, Spring Break Fever!, Good to be Bad! From the absence of literary quotations, I guessed that Shauna wasn't an English major, but there was nothing up on the wall to give a clue as to her larger interests or concerns. Or maybe there was: Party! Good to be Bad!

Most important was what I couldn't see. There were no plants! There was no delicate orchid that needed watering. This was not a gardening excursion. Shauna had brought me back for just one thing.

"You know, I liked you the first time I saw you," she said, slipping off her jacket.

"Hmmm?" I asked, throwing my own jacket on hers.

"Yeah," she said. "You're kind of cute and kind of thoughtful."

"And you're just wonderful," I sighed, "in every possible way."

Did I believe that? Of course not. I knew that Shauna was cute, that she had a good colour sense for decorating, and that she liked to make cutout collages. So "wonderful in every possible way" was a bit of hyperbole, but the words had good effect.

In a flash, Shauna was in my arms. We were kissing again, frantically, and then we somehow slipped down onto her bed. Shauna pulled back for a second, catching her breath.

"Music?" she asked, somewhat breathless. "I think we should have some music. Now what would you like?"

"Whatever you like," I replied.

"No, really," she said, running one finger up and down my chest.

"The Thinkertoys," I said.

"Your wish is my command," Shauna replied. Then she climbed off the bed, looked through a CD rack, and put on a two-year-old Thinkertoys disk, *Existential Epistles*, one of my favourites. *This girl is wonderful*, I said to myself.

"That should put you in the mood," she said, rejoining me on the bed.

"I'm already in the mood," I replied, as we began making out again.

The process of taking off a girl's clothes is truly an art, and one that I have yet to master. There is, of course, the question of timing. How fast should the clothes be unbuttoned and cast aside? In movies, the rip-and-rut mode seems to work for couples who are overcome with mutual lust, but in real life the lust is never that obvious. A guy has to look for clues and signals; he has to interpret signs and sighs and gestures that might mean start or stop or yield.

Shauna was quite wonderful at giving signals; in fact, all I had to do was follow her lead. She flicked open two buttons on my shirt, then began to toy with my rather hairless chest. I took this as an invitation to undo a couple of buttons on her shirt and, meeting no opposition, decided to continue this unbuttoning all the way down.

This brought me to an important juncture. I could, for instance, continue moving down to unzip her jeans, but that's both difficult (girls' jeans are ridiculously tight) and sometimes leads to a dead stop. Conversely, I could reach around and try to unhook her bra, a task always fraught with difficulty. Still, the prospect of flesh-on-flesh contact made me choose the second course.

Bra hooks! I believe bra hooks are among the most fiendish devices ever invented. I cannot figure out how girls manage to do them up, backwards, or reaching over or around or whatever they do, and I cannot figure out how girls ever manage to undo them. In my—admittedly limited—experience, bra hooks have always defeated me. I have heard guys boast that they can unhook a bra with one hand, or that there's some trick with two fingers that will pop the two, three, or four clasps that seem permanently hooked back there, but I cannot make that boast nor do I know that trick. Instead, after fumbling with one hand and getting nowhere, I reached awkwardly around Shauna with two hands and managed to unhook perhaps two of the three clasps that held the smooth cotton over her breasts. The pressure on the remaining clasp made it literally impossible to unhook.

Then, *magic*.

"Oh, here," Shauna said, reaching around to unhook the remaining clasp herself.

I responded in a very obvious way.

"Is it getting painful down there?" Shauna giggled, running her hand over my pants. "Maybe I can help."

And then she unzipped me.

"I see you like me," Shauna observed.

"Oh, yes," was all I could say.

At this point, the rest of our clothes got to the floor pretty quickly. Shirt, pants, underwear . . . they all came off in a flash. At the end, I had on nothing but my socks.

I caught a glimpse of myself in the mirror—a guy naked from his head to his ankles, but still wearing socks. I became aware that my socks were not attractive, and might even be mismatched.

Shauna was giving me an appraising look. She was not focused directly on my socks, but eyeballing me in a more general way. I became aware that my physique did not measure up to the fashion clips on her poster board, that my abs were not washboard but more like Bristol board, that my pecs were both pale and underdeveloped. And I was still wearing my socks.

In that fraction of a second, something changed between us. We had been headed in a particular direction, with a very obvious and desired conclusion, but somehow that forward movement came to a stop. A strange expression appeared in Shauna's eyes as she looked at me, a look that would have revealed something going on in her mind, had I been able to read it. As it was, I had to wait for some words.

"Wait," she said.

"Wait?" I repeated. Maybe I should just quickly pull off my socks and get on with this.

"Yeah, wait. You seem to think you're going to get some?" she asked.

I replied with my usual suave articulation. "Well, I, uh . . ."

"You're like all the other guys," she sighed, looking away. "You just want one thing. You think I'm so easy that you can get me in the sack, just like that."

"Well, I, uh . . ." I said, repeating myself.

"You guys are all the same," she sighed. "You think you're so wonderful and so irresistible and really you're just like all the others."

"Well, I, uh . . ." I seemed to have forgotten all the other words in the language.

"So just forget it," she said, sitting up. She reached over beside the bed and grabbed a nightshirt. In no time, it was over her head and covering that fabulous body. "That's enough."

"Was it the socks?" I asked.

"No, it's nothing. I changed my mind, that's all," Shauna said.

For a brief moment, as we looked at each other, while I tried to decide whether she was serious or just teasing me. I flashed a hopeful and perhaps engaging smile, but the look on her face was stern. It was time to begin putting my clothes back on.

I carefully retrieved my underwear and managed to pull them up and over the offending part of my anatomy, which was shrinking, but still ready for another change of mind.

"You guys . . ." Shauna began as I put on my clothes. It was the beginning of a lengthy monologue on men, our devious ways, our sexual urges, our misreading of the female mind. I wish I could remember it all, because there might have been clues there as to what went wrong, what I did or what I didn't do, but I was feeling pretty stupid and pretty awkward at this point so I was mostly focused on getting dressed. Men are quite vulnerable when they're naked. We may even be vulnerable with our clothes on, but at least it isn't quite so obvious.

When I was dressed, I apologized a couple of times for whatever I had done, or not done, or thought about doing. Then I said goodnight, and bent forward to give her a quick kiss. Shauna turned her cheek so I ended up kissing a mouthful of hair.

"Uh, can I call you?" I asked.

"Maybe," she said, looking back at me. "I have my moods, you know."

"I kind of gathered that," I replied.

She shot me a look, a pretty nasty look, as I slunk out of the room.

6

Prayers

IT MUST HAVE BEEN the socks. A guy who's about to have sex should always take off his socks so he doesn't end up looking ridiculous and ruining the mood. I was doing okay, really, until the socks. I was ready for takeoff, in launch position, but then Shauna saw my socks and it was launch aborted. Simple as that.

No, it couldn't be that simple. It must have been something I said, some gesture I made that killed the mood. What had I said? Something like, "Well, I, uh." That was pretty innocuous. Maybe it was *too* innocuous. Maybe I should have said something witty or seductive or romantic. Maybe I should have said, "My dear, you are a dream come true," or "You look better with your clothes off than with your clothes on." No, scratch that. Better to mumble "Well, I, uh" and adore her with my eyes.

I was halfway to my dorm when the scariest idea came to me: maybe I'm kind of repulsive with my clothes off. Maybe there's something about my body that just turns girls off. Maybe I should be working out in the gym, the way Kirk does, and building up my pecs and abs so I looked like one of the models on Shauna's bulletin board. Maybe a toned body really does make a difference.

Got to start working out, I said to myself.

With that resolve, I turned the key in the lock and walked into our dorm room. The room was dark so at first I saw nothing, but then I heard a strange noise. It sounded like sobbing. So I turned on my desk lamp and saw where the sobbing came from.

The sound was from my roommate, Kirk. He was on his knees, hands clasped, praying. There were tears running down his cheeks.

I panicked. In my family we do not display emotion. I have never seen either of my parents cry, or get terrifically excited, or show any emotion beside bland good spirits. I'm not even sure if we Macklins are capable of any big emotions, though I'm certainly making progress learning about frustration and depression.

But Kirk was obviously in the throes of some big emotion, some tremendous spiritual upheaval. Why else would he be on his knees? Why else would he be crying? Surely I had to do something to help him.

"Kirk," I asked in a whisper. "Are you alright?"

He looked up. His face was as pathetic as any I have ever seen, as if he had just been witness to all the sufferings of the world.

"I'm lost," he cried. "I'm a fallen man." His voice was raspy, as if he'd been weeping for hours.

"It's not that bad," I said, just to be comforting. Actually, I had no idea how bad it might be, or even what the "it" was.

"It *is* bad," he said. "It's terrible. I've betrayed myself, and God, and my parents, and Kathy, and everything I believe in."

That was quite a list. I stayed quiet.

He looked up at me. "I was tested tonight, Al. I was tested—my resolve was tested, my faith was tested—and I was found wanting. I was weak . . . weak!"

By now, my curiosity was piqued. When last I saw my roommate, he was happily dancing with a gaggle of girls at Butter. How could all this testing and weakness have happened in the course of a couple of hours? So I asked the obvious question.

"What did you do?"

There was a pause. He looked at me, angrily, then down at his chest, even more angrily.

"You left me alone with her, Al. You thought I was strong. You thought I could resist her, but I wasn't ready. I didn't know how."

"Rachel?" I asked.

"Or Eve or Delilah," Kirk went on. "Temptation has so many names, so many disguises. I should have been ready, Al. I should have seen what she was up to, but I gave in to temptation."

My mind leapt forward, or backward, but certainly made a jump. "Did you get laid?" The words just blurted out of my mouth.

Kirk got to his feet, shaking his head and looking at me angrily. "Don't be crude," he snapped. "I may be weak, but I am not corrupt. Please, Al!"

"Sorry," I said, and I truly was, "but the way you were talking I kind of, well, kind of thought the worst. I'm glad it wasn't that bad." These words sounded quite strange coming from my lips, but they seemed the right thing at the moment.

Again there was a pause. There seemed to be some tremendous emotion welling up inside of Kirk, like he was getting ready to explode. His mouth opened slightly, his eyes stared forward like a man on the edge of sanity. "She kissed me!" he spat out, and then he covered his face and dissolved into sobs.

I guess I could have put my arm around him, but I have so little experience with real emotion that I decided to keep my arm where it was. Words, I thought, words can be a solace.

"Well, that's not so bad," I told him. "You can't be responsible for what somebody else does. I mean, you're a handsome guy, Kirk, and girls are going to do things like that. You can't control what other people are going to do. Your only real control is over what you do."

He pulled one hand down from his face and looked at me, despondent. "I kissed her back," he whispered. Then the tears started again.

I could have said something, I suppose, but my little speeches hadn't worked that well so far. Who was I to demean the importance of a kiss? Sure, for most guys—for me—a kiss was next to nothing; it was first base in the metaphorical ball game, and you didn't really score until you got to home plate. But I couldn't say that. I couldn't tell Kirk that a kiss was just a kiss, I mean, that would be like singing the old song from *Casablanca*.

"Well, Kathy doesn't have to know about it," I said. "You made a mistake, now just move on." That was always the approach in our family: sweep problems under the metaphorical rug.

"I can't," Kirk said, sniffling. "I promised to be true to her. We promised to be open with each other."

"Well, uh, in that case . . ." I began, my words falling off because I had no idea what to say. Instead, I grabbed a Kleenex and handed it to my roommate. "Here, this might help," I said.

"Thanks," he replied, blowing his nose. "I know you can't understand this, Al, but it's like the fall of man, like Adam and the forbidden fruit."

This is, like, too melodramatic, is what I thought to myself. I have no particular expertise in theology, but it seems to me that kissing a girl who's already in the process of kissing you is pretty low on the order of sins. Besides, I had my own problems to think about and was getting a little tired of Kirk's carrying on.

"Kirk, if you keep talking like that, you won't have a prayer of getting over this."

He looked at me suddenly, with bright eyes. "Prayer? Were you offering to pray with me?"

That wasn't what I said, but obviously Kirk found the idea appealing.

"Would you?" he asked, his face beaming.

I sighed. "For you, Kirk, as a special favour."

For a second, I was afraid he might hug me, but that moment passed and all I got was a deep "thank you." Then Kirk closed his eyes and began, I suppose, to pray.

Now I was a bit confused since I didn't know much about religion or prayer or anything like that. At my house, we never even said grace before meals and I'd only been to church for my granddad's funeral, so I was more than a little inexperienced at this.

"Do we kneel, or anything?" I asked.

"No," Kirk replied, "just close your eyes and send your thoughts to God."

This was a bit disappointing. At least at my granddad's church there were a few inspiring things to look at: statues, stained glass windows, and plaques on the walls commemorating the death of the Very Reverend So-and-so who faithfully served the flock from

1872 to 1896. But Kirk and I were in our dorm room, so inspiration was limited. Better to close my eyes, I suppose, than stare at a blank TV screen.

So I offered up a prayer. *Dear God,* I said to myself, *please forgive my friend for his trivial sin and let him go back to the righteous, guilt-free life he ordinarily lives. He's a decent guy and deserves a break.* That was pretty much my only request on the issue, so I opened one eye only to find Kirk still lost in prayer.

I closed that eye and decided to keep going. Since I was asking God on Kirk's behalf, maybe I should ask something for me, too. *Dear God,* I went on, *please let me succeed in my simple and admittedly mundane goals, because not all of us are as lofty as your servant Kirk. Please let Shauna forgive me, despite my mismatched socks and repulsive body, and let her change her mind once again so that your servant, Al, who has spent so many years trying to get laid, can finally succeed in his quest.*

"Thank you," Kirk said when I opened my eyes this time. "Prayer is a wonderful thing."

"Let us hope," I sighed. "Let us hope."

7

The Grind

I BELIEVE KIRK'S PRAYERS were answered. He awoke at dawn the next morning, as he did most mornings, but spent a full two hours at the gym rather than the usual one. I believe he might have been "mortifying the flesh," something that medieval monks used to do when they sinned. Later, he had a long phone call with Kathy, punctuated with sighs and tears and earnest expressions of love—at least from what I could hear as I paced the hall—and he emerged forgiven by the girl of his dreams.

The good Lord, I suspect, is kind to the truly faithful.

The good Lord, however, doesn't pay much attention to the odd prayer from some poor sinner who's been left with an embarrassing physical condition and only a pair of socks on his feet. Though I called Shauna's cell phone five times, and left messages that ranged from pathetic apology to annoyed why-aren't-you-calling-me, it was obvious that I'd been ditched.

This might not have been so terrible if I'd known exactly why. Unfortunately, I couldn't really discuss with Kirk what had happened, since it was too far beyond his experience, and I couldn't very well explain it in an email to Maggie, who, whether I had on socks or not, had managed to resist having sex with me for our entire last year of high school. Still, I could hint at the issue.

From: amacklin@BU.edu
To: maggiemac@sl.edu
Serious question: how important is it for a guy to have a really hot body? Maybe you could survey the girls in

your dorm and let me know the consensus. Lately I'm feeling a bit unattractive, verging on repulsive. My roommate works out in the gym every morning. Should I wake up early and join him?

From: maggiemac@sl.edu
To: amacklin@BU.edu
Sounds like you had a really great time at that dance club. But relax, Al, there's nothing wrong with your body. You're even quite attractive in a kind of skinny, hairless way. I didn't have to do a survey to answer your question: a hot body doesn't matter all that much. If it did, Bill Gates would still be a single geek. Those guys who work out in the gym all day should try reading a book or two. I go for attractive minds; washboard abs actually look kind of bizarre.

Maggie's email was encouraging, but I continued to mull over the issue. Unfortunately, I am not good at mulling. Sometimes I think I am not capable of extended thought. The television programmers who insert commercials every eleven minutes have got it right—eleven minutes is a lot of sustained attention. I know guys who have trouble with concentrating even that long, but I vowed to at least hit the average. Surely any serious issue deserves some mulling time.

So I mulled over my failure with Shauna for a number of eleven-minute segments over the course of a week, and then decided that I had made no real gain in understanding. Maybe it was me; maybe it was her; maybe it was the socks. I would never know.

What I did know at the end of that week was more mundane: Psychology 101 was killing me. I had taken the course with good intentions—everybody should know a little psychology, I thought—but the lectures were really heavy on experiments with mice, electric shocks, and little rewards of mouse-food. I tried, for a while, to develop some interest in the poor, tortured, and confused mice, or to see some connection between mice and men, like that famous book by somebody-or-other, but I was getting nowhere. The lecture class was enormous, the professor had a voice like a flatulent goose, and the textbook was going to set me back $125. I managed to get along by using Kirk's textbook for the first couple of weeks, but when my first multiple-choice came back with a miserable thirty-two inscribed by the computer scorer, I knew it was time to act.

At the beginning of drop-and-add week, I made an appointment at the Dean's Office to change the course. Drop-and-add week is the last chance to scoot out of a course before a dismal mark appears on your transcript. At the same time, it was my last chance to add a course that might actually interest me. So on the last week of September, I waited outside the Dean's Office to meet with G. M. Thayer, the dean assigned to first-year M's like me.

"Mr. Macklin?"

I looked up, but saw no one who appeared at all deanish. There was a short, rather attractive woman with dark hair standing at the door amid a dozen students, waiting for their chance to drop and add.

"Alan Macklin . . ."

The voice was coming from the short, rather attractive woman. "Yes, right here."

"Come this way," she replied with a smile.

It was quite a lovely smile, really, quite warm and full of character. One of her teeth was slightly twisted, and a bottom tooth slightly discoloured, but that just made her smile seem real. I hate people with magazine smiles: with perfect, identical white teeth. Ms. Thayer had a real smile, so I was sure that she'd okay my course change.

I followed her through a mouse-maze of cubicles, wondering if an electric shock or a little piece of grain was waiting for me at the end. Instead, I found myself in a tiny half-office that had three chairs, a computer, and a bookshelf.

"What can we do for you, Alan?" she asked, flashing that genuine smile one more time.

"Well, I'm having a little trouble in Pysch," I said. "So I was wondering if I could drop the course and maybe pick up something a little more in line with, uh . . ." My words dropped off, as they sometimes do when my thoughts run a little ahead of them. My thoughts, at that moment, were engaged in some interesting speculation on just how attractive Dean Thayer happened to be, and how much more attractive she might be with a little less clothing. It took some willpower to snap my mind back to reality.

"Drop and add," she said, looking at the computer screen. "Looks like Psychology 101 isn't for you."

"It's not that I haven't been trying," I began. "And I'm sure the course will get more interesting later on, but, frankly, I'm not doing that well with this behaviourist stuff."

Her brown eyes looked at the screen, then back at me. "A thirty-two on the first quiz."

I smiled, a fairly genuine smile, right back to her. "Aren't computers wonderful?"

"Your other marks are quite good, Alan," she said. "You're getting an A in Poetry and Short Fiction, and your Humanities mark is good."

"Thank you, Dean Thayer."

"Gloria," she said, smiling again. "I'm not a dean, just an admin. assistant. We help out during drop-and-add week."

"Aha," I said. "I had a hunch you were too good-looking to be a dean."

She groaned. "Let's get down to business, Alan. What course were you thinking of adding?"

"I was wondering about Women in Modern Society," I said. "The course description looked kind of interesting."

"Looking to meet some girls, eh?" she asked wryly.

I kept my mouth shut. Of course I was out to meet some girls. Why else would I sign up for a course in the women's studies department? But there was no way I could respond to her question with a truthful answer.

"Let me see," Ms. Thayer said, typing something into the computer. "There's room. Is that the course you really want?" Her middle finger hovered over the enter key, waiting for me to say something.

"Well, I suppose," I said.

Her finger dropped. "Done." She looked up. "Anything else you'd like?"

Now that question sent my mind leaping. Ms. Call-me-Gloria Thayer seemed even more attractive because she was so matter-of-fact. There was something about her no-nonsense attitude that was getting me positively excited, but I pushed that thought aside and wiggled in the chair.

"No, not really, but I was just wondering," I said, "if anyone ever told you how much you look like Ashley Judd."

She shot me a look that did not come with a smile. "Just my ex-husband," she said. "And he was a jerk."

And that, as they say, was that.

Walking back to the dorm, I spent the next eleven minutes wondering if I, too, might be a jerk. I wondered if my shallowness and my lack of direction might make me a jerk, or my lack of sensitivity, or my general cloddishness. I wondered if I might have gotten laid by now if I were not a jerk, or at least managed to hide my jerkishness.

All those questions were spinning through my mind when I got back to our dorm room. Kirk was reading a book, something serious and unjerkish, and looked up.

"Am I a jerk?" I asked him.

He gave me a look. "Somebody suggest that?" he asked.

"Kind of, and I've been wondering."

"Hmmm," he said, like a doctor considering a patient. "Let me just check." He grabbed a dictionary from his bookshelf. "*Webster's* says that a jerk is 'a stupid, dull, and fatuous person.'" I don't think you fit the bill. You're definitely not stupid, since your marks are mostly okay, and at least a few people think you're interesting."

"What about fatuous?"

"Got to look that one up," he said. "Hmmm, it means 'silly and pointless.'" He gave me a searching look. "I have known you to be silly, and maybe lacking direction."

"So I *am* fatuous," I sighed.

"But not a jerk."

These are the kind of intellectual discussions that we're supposed to have at university, discussions that suggest the great traditions of thought and philosophy which lie at the basis of our culture. I'm sure that my parents, had they heard this learned back-and-forth, would have felt reassured that their tuition money was being well spent. I'm sure that Maggie, even in her Ivy League school, would have had to acknowledge that there was some intellectual depth out here at BU. If my attention span could actually extend beyond eleven minutes, we might have delved further into some serious self-examination.

As it was, the eleven minutes was up. "Let's go eat," I said.

Kirk had become my best friend at school despite the enormous differences in our interests and backgrounds. He was cleaner, neater, and more conscientious than I was. On the other hand, I brought a certain amount of disorder and zaniness to his otherwise serious life, a *je ne sais quoi*, you might say. While Kirk would neatly press his own shirts (and mine, if I asked him), I would be the one to show him that boxer shorts actually exist and that a guy could wear a shirt without an undershirt beneath it. One day, I even showed Kirk that the Internet was not a den of sin and iniquity, that websites like the fan site for the Thinkertoys did not have pictures of nude women. Another day we went over to Fuji's room and I showed him that not all video games were filled with violence, blood, and gore.

We balanced each other, Kirk and I. We even had a few courses in common—Humanities 101 and Poetry and Short Fiction 105 among them. Kirk was better in Humanities with his knowledge of the Bible and his feel for Greek philosophy. I was stronger in English, always my best subject, though I was having some trouble when we got to Milton's *Paradise Lost,* and we just couldn't agree on whether Satan or God was the more interesting character. Still, our discussions were invigorating, perhaps more so because we had such different ideas.

It's possible that our debates were having some effect on me. At least Maggie thought so.

To: amacklin@BU.edu
From: maggiemac@sl.edu
Your last email sounded almost intellectual. When did this nasty trend get started? I expect you to stay the same adorable idiot you've always been, and suddenly you're writing about Satan and original sin. I think this Christian roommate is starting to get to you. Next thing you know, they'll start dunking you in water and declaring you born again. Wasn't being born once trouble enough?

Actually, I don't think Kirk was getting to me as much as the entire place. Somebody wrote in our school paper that going off to university had much in common with going to jail. We're cut off from our friends and families, put in an overcrowded environment, consistently belittled by our guards/professors, and forced to rethink all our ideas and values. In a prison, the inmates suck up to guards for a few smokes; here we suck up to professors for an extra three marks on an assignment.

I thought that article was a little over the top, since our suffering and overcrowding here at BU were hardly on the level of Kingston Pen, but the attitude change was scarily real. In this tiny, cloistered (another good word!) environment, nothing outside of the campus seems very important.

So I was saying to Kirk. We sat eating lunch at the sundial one day near the end of October. It was a glorious day: the sun shining brightly in a crisp blue sky, a few fallen leaves blowing gently across the crowd, and everyone enjoying the warmth enough to strip off coats and heavy sweaters.

"A day like this is a gift, Al," Kirk said, leaning back on the concrete. "A gift from—"

"God," I said, filling in. I was watching the various coeds and secretaries parade across campus and, frankly, God was the last thing on my mind.

"Ah, you're finally figuring it out."

"I just know how you think."

"And I know what you're thinking about," he replied. "Either the blonde over there by the fence, or the girl with short hair and the big, uh, you know."

"Did you actually suggest what I thought you did?"

Kirk refused to comment. Of course, he was right. I was looking at the blonde by the fence *and* the dark-haired girl with big boobs. I was admiring the dark-haired girl, especially, when I realized that I had met her before.

"Where are you going?" Kirk asked.

"Got to talk to an old friend," I told him.

8

Gloriana

It had been almost a month since the fiasco with Shauna. I had decided, after her, to give up on women and concentrate on my studies. This resolve was made more more difficult by the hundreds of attractive women in my various courses. My new women's studies course, for instance, was a virtual gold mine of glittering girls. I could, I suppose, have asked any of them to go out for coffee, or go to a club, or join me at Slavin Hall for lunch. But I didn't. I was studying. Perhaps I was in a fallow period, just waiting for the moment to begin again.

But when I saw Gloria Thayer eating her lunch by the concrete railing outside Randolf Hall, I was reminded just how attractive she was.

I walked up beside her and propped my arms on the railing.

"Ms. Thayer, I was wrong," I began. "You do not look like Ashley Judd. You look better than that. I'd say you look remarkably like yourself."

She turned and looked at me. Her face was quite perfect without any makeup at all. Just like her: no nonsense. The expression on that face was somewhere between neutral and moderately annoyed.

"It's Al Macklin," I said, continuing. "The jerk?"

"Oh, I remember," she said, blushing a little. "You were changing a course."

"Psychology to . . . remember?"

She studied my face for a second. "Women's studies, right?"

"Absolutely right. Your advice to go into that course was, well, genius. I don't know how to thank you."

I could see her wondering whether she had actually given me that advice, but I decided not to give her too long to reflect. When chatting up a girl, it's important to keep the patter going.

"I can see now that my Ashley Judd comment was totally inappropriate. That kind of comparison is demeaning because of its emphasis on the physical. See, that's just one of the things I've learned in that new course. Women have been objectified for centuries by a male-dominated culture, so really, it's no wonder you thought I was a jerk."

"I didn't call you a jerk, did I?" she asked.

"No, no," I said. "You'd never do something like that. It was just an offhand comparison with your ex-husband."

"Oh, *that* jerk."

"That fool is what I would say," I went on. "To lose a woman like you, a man would have to be an idiot." *What a line*, I said to myself. *How do I come up with these things? And why can't I find words like that when I really need them?*

"Come on, you don't even know me." She turned away and took a bite out of her sandwich.

"But I'd like to," I replied.

She turned back to me, trying to look miffed, but there was a smile underneath the annoyance. "Alan, I'm old enough to be, well, almost your mother."

"Not so," I told her. "I'm twenty," I said, exaggerating by a year or so, "and I suspect you're about thirty, so that's only ten years between us. Now there have been a couple recorded cases of ten year olds giving birth, but that's pretty rare."

"I'm thirty-two," she said.

"Still pretty rare," I came back. "What if I told you that I'm very mature for a twenty year old, that I'm really twenty going on thirty. Besides, what's a decade between friends?"

"I can't believe this. Are you actually coming on to me?"

I gave her my best Hugh Grant look. "Actually, yes. I am."

We had reached a pretty tense moment, a moment of decision. Gloria could, for instance, take her sandwich and smoosh it into my face, then go stomping off to her office. She could, on the other hand, continue the dalliance by asking me just what I had in mind. *Dalliance*, isn't that a great word? These days we have too much hooking up and not enough dalliance.

I could see on her face the various thoughts that must have been going through her mind. I was a kid, that was true, but not that much of a kid. She was older, that was true, but not that much older. Did she have a boyfriend? Was she still carrying a thing for "the jerk" ex-husband? Was there some university policy against admin. assistants going out with students? Lots of thoughts to consider in perhaps five seconds. It gave a person some respect for the human brain.

"This is crazy," she said. But I caught the smile.

"Sensible is overrated," I replied. "How about we have lunch tomorrow?"

Gloria gave me an appraising look. Would I just go away if she told me to? Did she really want me to go away? There was another five seconds to consider things.

"Coffee," she said at last. "But not on campus. There's a Starbucks on Nanaimo Street. I'll meet you there for a few minutes after work, tomorrow about five."

I smiled and agreed, then she packed up her sandwich and headed back to the Dean's Office.

I stayed put until Kirk came up beside me. I tried to keep a poker face rather than asking immediately for a high-five. Then again, I'm not sure Kirk knew how to do a high-five.

"So how'd you do?" he asked.

"Coffee date, tomorrow," I said, breaking into a wide grin.

"Pretty smooth, Al. Remind me to take lessons from you if I ever have to look for a girl."

"From what I can tell," I replied, "you need lessons in how to fight them off."

I admit I was a bit nervous about meeting Gloria for coffee. I have done a few coffee dates over the last couple of years, but this was my first experience ever with an "older woman." In my film course, the "older woman" was a stock character in the old Hollywood movies. Actresses like Jane Wyman created such roles. Anne Bancroft seduced a very young Dustin Hoffman in *The Graduate*, a movie that was popular about twenty years before I was born. But these older women really were older, like in their forties, while Gloria was only *somewhat* older. Still, she was definitely more experienced than me—she'd been married, she might even have kids! For a few minutes, while I sat in the Film 101 lab watching *Gone with the Wind* clips, I felt positively terrified. It was only a couple years ago that I started going out with sixteen year olds; now I was doubling the age factor.

As the question goes, what was I thinking?

Nevertheless, it was too late to back down. Given my luck over the past little while, it would probably all come to nothing. So after class I headed over to the Starbucks on Nanaimo Street. It was a rainy afternoon, and the general gloom meshed with my hopeless mood. I was early, of course, so I got my grande latte, and sat on one of two stools at a small table, and waited. And waited. And waited. I checked my watch every five minutes, then began to wonder if I had the wrong date or the wrong Starbucks. I eventually asked the counter guy if there was another Starbucks on Nanaimo, but he said I was at the one and only. By five-thirty, my latte was cold and I had decided that Gloria had simply changed her mind. Part of me was disappointed, but part of me was exhaling sighs of relief. What had I been thinking?

I was at the door, heading out, when Gloria came rushing in.

"Sorry," she said, closing her umbrella. "I got held up."

"No problem," I lied.

"Let me buy you something," she offered, by way of apology.

So I asked for an espresso, since that seemed a bit more mature than the latte I had just finished, and Gloria got a straight black coffee. We settled back at the small table I had just abandoned and talked small: weather, lateness, apologies.

"I can't believe I agreed to meet you here," Gloria said. "The administration frowns on this kind of thing."

"What kind of thing?"

"Staff and students, seeing each other," she said. "You could haul me up on harassment charges."

"But I haven't been harassed."

"So far I've managed to control myself." She laughed.

I liked the sound of that remark. Gloria was looking quite, well, glorious that afternoon, even after a long day at the Dean's Office. Her hair shone under the lights, her smile flashed, her eyes sparkled. I would not have minded her harassing me at all, but that seemed a pretty remote possibility.

We had only twenty minutes to talk that afternoon. I found out that there *were* children, ages three and seven, waiting at home with a babysitter. I found out that Gloria had graduated from BU ten years ago, gotten married, then taken a part-time job at the Dean's Office that had turned into a full-time job after her divorce. "Happens," she said with a shrug.

I'm not sure what Gloria found out about me. She had already seen my class schedule, and talking about my classes to someone ten years beyond all that seemed a bit juvenile. So I talked about my home town, about movies, about my roommate Kirk, and about poetry. I tried not to sound like a kid. *Be mature*, I told myself. *Pretend you're mature*.

Then we reached that awkward moment when Gloria had to go—was this going forward or coming to a quick end? Usually, a guy gets a sense of his prospects long before the coffees are finished, but I really didn't have a clue. There were no signs, no quick touches of hands, or smiles, or shared laughter. Maybe older women are like that, a little more secretive. I had to ask.

"Can I see you again?"

She gave me a serious look. "So you're not scared off? An older woman with kids and emotional baggage from a lousy marriage, and you still want to go out?"

"Yeah, I do."

She shook her head. "Here, email me," she said, scribbling her address on a piece of paper. "I've got to run."

The next day, I sent one email, which got a very quick reply.

> From: amacklin@BU.edu
> To: glthayer@cyberthorn.com
> Thanks for the coffee. I really enjoyed seeing you this afternoon. Can we get together again sometime soon?

> From: glthayer@cyberthorn.com
> To: amacklin@BU.edu
> Glutton for punishment? If you help me take the kids around for Halloween trick-or-treats, I'll reward you with dinner. Let me know.

9

Trick and Treat

I WAS DOING UP my makeup when Kirk saw me in the bathroom. I had just finished turning my face a rather pukey green and was now adding some appropriate drips of blood to the corner of my mouth.

"Nice costume," he quipped. "What are you?"

"A ghoul."

"That should really impress Gloria's children," he said. "Why couldn't you go as a cowboy or a prince?"

"Those costumes weren't on sale at Wal-Mart," I replied, picking up the headband-knife that completed my look. "You don't dress up for Halloween?"

"Halloween is a pagan holiday," Kirk told me. It was his serious I'm-going-to-be-a-minister voice.

"So you're going to a prayer meeting instead?" I asked.

"Don't be sarcastic," he said, before changing the subject. "Are you sure you're ready for this woman? I mean, she's almost old enough to be your mother." Same serious, I'm-going-to-be-a-minister voice.

"I've been through the math on that, and it's not true. Besides, this trick-or-treat thing could be fun. What's the alternative? Head off to a pathetic Halloween Dance at Slavin? Play video games with Fuji? As Keats once wrote, 'He ne'er is crowned with . . . ' uh, something or other . . . 'who fears to follow where his heart doth lead.'"

"Did he really write that?" Kirk knew that I tended to make up quotations.

"Something like that," I replied. "Anyhow, my heart leadeth me to Gloria's and perhaps some innocent gambol later in the evening. Pretty good word, *gambol,* eh? Anyhow, wish me luck."

Kirk did not wish me luck. I think he had some deep feeling of disapproval for sin and people like me who are desperately trying to sin. If only I were more successful at sinning, perhaps I'd be worthy of his scorn.

I headed across campus in my outfit, dressed for Halloween a bit earlier in the evening than anyone else, garnering a few smiles as I went. Little kids go out trick-or-treating early these days for fear of the various evildoers who hit the streets at, say, seven o'clock. I had agreed to be at Gloria's house at five-thirty, and that meant getting on a city bus at five o'clock. The various commuters on the number 13 bus gave this ghoul an amused look as I boarded, then returned to the vacant stares that are appropriate to bus travel. I had to stand most of the way, which is difficult for a man with a fake knife in his head, but I survived.

Following Gloria's directions, I made my way into a set of winding subdivision streets until I reached her house. It was a pleasant bungalow done up in a fake-brick finish with a very large garage fronting on the street. It was basically identical to every third house in the subdivision, the other two-thirds boasting somewhat different fronts and even larger garages.

I rang the bell. I heard thudding footsteps from one of the kids, and then the front door flew open.

It was the three year old, a cute little blonde girl who was half-dressed in her fairy costume. She looked at me with wide eyes.

I smiled back.

And then she screamed "Mommy!" and burst into tears.

A fine start, I said to myself, removing the fake knife from my head.

Gloria's son reached the door, a seven year old with an adolescent's attitude. "Nice ghoul outfit, guy."

"Thank you," I replied, somewhat humbled.

Gloria finally appeared, holding the tear-filled child in one arm. "Alan, I'm so sorry. Lexy is so sensitive."

"I'm just a person, see?" I said, smiling my very best human smile at the girl. "Just a guy."

Little Lexy hid her face in her mother's shoulder.

"I'm Brad," said her brother. Then he looked up at his sister. "She cries all the time, for nothing."

"Well, maybe my costume is too scary."

He gave me an appraising look. "You're not scary. Besides, I saw the costume at *Wal-Mart* last week. It was in the cheap bin."

Should have gone for the cowboy outfit, I said to myself.

"Bradley, that's quite enough," Gloria told him sternly. Then she turned to me. "Just give us a little time to get ready, and off we go."

The three of them went off upstairs to where I suspected the bedrooms were. That left me alone, with a chance to look around the house. The furniture was very much like that at my parents' house, but a bit more stained from various colours of baby food. The fireplace looked like it hadn't been used for a while, the windows had little fingerprints at the Lexy level. There were pictures on various side tables: baby photos, Brad in a baseball outfit looking displeased, Lexy in a little dress looking adorable, the three of them together on a picnic, probably taken by the now-absent dad.

I wandered out to the kitchen and found the fridge entirely covered with shopping lists (Cheerios figured prominently), reminders of hockey practices and dental appointments, magnets with various logos and designs ("Bill Starr can sell your house. Remember, he's a star!"), magnetic letters spelling out "Brad is way cool" and still more photos. Some of these were ripped photographs that must have once contained the ex-husband. Now his image was gone and only Gloria and the kids were shown. Mr. Thayer, if that was his name, apparently had not left under amicable circumstances.

"We're ready," Gloria announced from the front hall.

Indeed they were. Gloria was dressed as a princess, complete with a crown. Little Lexy was a fairy of some sort, with a gossamer outfit and a sparkling magic wand. Bradley was dressed in the cowboy outfit I was too cheap to buy. He looked angry.

"I don't want to be a cowboy," he whined. "I want to be a gangsta."

"No gangstas in this house," Gloria told him. "You can be a cowboy or you can be a kid stuck in his room all Halloween. Got it?"

This tough choice managed to stop the whining. The kids grabbed their trick-or-treat bags and led us out the door.

"I'm sorry about Bradley," Gloria whispered to me when the kids were safely ahead of us. "He's been pretty awful lately."

"He's not that bad," I lied. "And it must be tough to be a single mom, or should I say a single princess?"

She laughed, very princess-like, as the kids ran up to their first house. This trick-or-treat proved to be quite a success, with a decent-sized Snickers bar plopped in each of their bags.

So we traipsed from house to house, collecting whatever goodies were offered, admiring the carved pumpkins and the occasional elaborate Halloween display of ghouls, goblins, and flashing lights. Somebody once calculated that people spend more money on Halloween than on any holiday except Christmas, and Halloween isn't even a holiday! Go figure.

The hour we spent on the streets went reasonably well, I thought. Little Lexy fell down only once and burst into frightened tears no more than five times during our walk through the neighbourhood. Boisterous Brad began sneak-eating his candies about halfway along, but we pretended not to notice. He was mostly cheerful, with only the occasional grousing when someone would give him something healthy to eat. "Raisins! What kind of person gives a kid raisins?"

When we returned to the house, Gloria had the kids select five candies each and then gave them permission to plop in front of the TV to watch a video until seven-thirty. I washed off my makeup and returned, as best I could, to my usual Alan Macklin look. Gloria took off her princess costume and emerged in a jeans and T-shirt outfit that fit her very well indeed. Then the two of us went off to the kitchen to prepare dinner.

"I hope spaghetti and a salad is okay," she said. "I'm not much of a cook, really."

"It'll be great. Anything beats the food at Slavin. And it'll go with the red wine I brought."

"The corkscrew is in the drawer," she said. "How about you pour and I'll begin the lengthy preparation of authentic Italian spaghetti sauce."

She got out a jar of Ragu while I fished for a wine opener, finding only some stainless steel device that looked vaguely like a rabbit. It occurred to me, then, that I had never actually opened a bottle of wine before, even with a regular corkscrew. I picked the rabbit-thing up, stared at it, flipped it in several directions, but didn't have a clue where to start. It seemed to me that this might be an omen of the evening to come.

"Oh, here, I'll do it," Gloria said when she had the sauce on the stove. With a quick zip, flip and pull, she had the cork out and sitting in her fingertips. "Would you like to sniff the cork, monsieur?" she asked.

"*Certainement*," I said, remembering one word from high school French. Then I went on in my best Pepé Le Pew accent. "It smells—'ow you zay in Eenglish?—like cork."

Gloria laughed and poured. We toasted and sipped. Then she started some water boiling and opened a package of salad. "Let me just get the kids to bed. I'll need a couple minutes to read them a story."

"I'll stir the sauce," I said, pouring myself a little more wine.

I sat on a bar stool in the kitchen, sipping wine and stirring the spaghetti sauce, feeling warm and pleased and very mature. This was so, so *domestic*. Maybe this older woman thing really worked for me; maybe I was just too mature for young university girls in their pink dorm rooms. Maybe I was destined to be with older women in their taupe-coloured suburban homes, sipping their wine, waiting for them to be ready for me . . . the younger man.

Finally Gloria returned. She looked more beautiful than ever to my wine-addled eyes.

"Did you leave any for me?" she asked, looking at the wine bottle.

"Oh, I, uh . . ." I replied.

She laughed and pulled another bottle from a shelf over the countertop. Then she threw in the spaghetti, and in a few minutes we were sitting down for dinner in the kitchen. Overhead, I could hear Brad—pumped up on Halloween candy—running back and forth. In front of me, however, was a very, very beautiful woman. I thought about that word, *woman*. I had been out with *girls* before this, with a half dozen different kinds of girls, but Gloria was my first *woman*. Or might be my first woman, if it all worked out.

"You know the funny thing," she said after dinner, when we were halfway into that second bottle of wine, "I was nervous about tonight."

"You're kidding," I said. "I'm the one who should be terrified."

"Yeah, right," she replied, the words coming out *yeahrright*. All our words were slurred now. Wine does that. "I haven't been out with a guy since I dated Geoff."

"The jerk," I said.

"Yeah, that guy. And here's my first date as an almost single person, and it's with a guy who's half my age.

I think I blushed.

Gloria reached out and touched my hand. "Sorry, I didn't mean that. It's just so strange, this whole thing. But you're a good guy, Al, really you are."

"Thank you," I said. "And you're wonderful."

I won't go on with more of this dialogue. Two people, wine sodden, sexually frustrated, vaguely interested . . . it just doesn't lead to literary talk. We probably sounded more like a snippet from *Days of Our Lives*, to tell the truth.

But I did get my first kiss in that kitchen, as part of that dialogue, and it was wonderful. I think older women are better at kissing: they know how to give a kiss just the right touch, just the right brush of lip against lip, just the right hint of more to come.

Then we went off to the family room to watch a DVD. Gloria offered me a choice of *Night of the Living Dead* or some movie with Richard Gere, so I decided to "pass on the gore and go for the Gere." Gloria laughed. After two bottles of wine, she found me funny and sweet and sexy. That's what she said—her exact words, almost.

We started making out after ten minutes of the movie. This was just like being in a real theatre, except that we were alone in the family room with no one to stare at us with disapproval, and only the vague anxiety that Lexy or Brad should wander down the stairs and interrupt us.

I can now report that older women also make out better than college girls. They know lots of different ways to kiss, lots of ways to get a guy excited, lots of ways to stretch out that excitement. They can even do all this with all their clothes on.

"So you're probably thinking that you're going to get some, aren't you?" Gloria said, pulling her lips back from mine.

I had heard this line only a month before, and that context was none too pleasant. "Well, I, uh. . ."

"Well, don't get your hopes up too soon. We've got to go slow on this," she said.

"Right."

"Slow means get your hand out from under my shirt."

"Uh, right."

"And slow means kiss me a lot."

"That works for me."

"And if you can count to three, Alan, you might just get what you really want."

10

Counting to Three

To: amacklin@BU.edu
From: maggiemac@sl.edu
What are these questions about older women? I am no longer your dating advisor, Al. If you feel like going out with the school secretaries, that's up to you. I promise you, I will not be jealous. I can understand your thinking, though. Frankly, I find older men a bit more attractive than my fellow first-years. I've got an invitation to go skiing in New Hampshire at Christmas with this grad student, and I'm toying with it. In the meanwhile, there's a book by Vizinczey called *In Praise of Older Women*. I haven't read it, but you might find the advice you need. Ciao.

I thought I detected a little jealousy in Maggie's email, and that gave me an ego boost. Maybe she still cared about me, just a little, or maybe she had always cared about me, but not enough. Still, I had to stay focused. My current goal was here, not on the other side of the continent, and for her I was counting to three. My second date with Gloria had consisted of cheering at Brad's hockey game, dinner at McDonald's, and some serious making out on the family room couch. Now I had reached the evening of date three, the end of the count, and I had to get ready. I selected a condom from the dozen left for me by my father, then thought briefly and took another. Who knew what kind of great lover I might prove to be under the expert guidance of Gloria Thayer?

Our third date actually involved going out, like a real date. Gloria got a babysitter, a girl named Donna who was roughly my age, and arranged for the two of us to have all of Saturday evening together. We went out for dinner at a fusion Thai–German restaurant (the sauerkraut had ginger in it and the sausages were made of duck), then off to a European film so serious that it made the syllabus of my film course look like fluff. We were still able to make out a little in the theatre, at least until the Nazi storm troopers arrived on screen. Nazi storm troopers, I have found, put a damper on romance.

What had I learned about Gloria Thayer from our three dates? I'd learned that her ex-husband had been an actor during his university days, appearing in bit parts in such epics as *Scream 2* (look for the guy in the clown mask) and *The Horror*, parts 3, 4, and 5 (look for the masked guy with the scary machete). When the big break into the majors did not appear, he abandoned acting and went into construction, something that apparently suited his threatening physique.

Gloria had begun working at the university to support her ex's film career, then kept on working even as he became quite successful in construction. Sadly, working with brick, concrete, and two-by-fours led to a personality change: the ex lost that artistic quality that first drew Gloria to him, and they began to wrangle. Wrangling turned to fighting and then more fighting, until one day Gloria walked out, taking the kids with her.

Apparently young Brad responded poorly to the split, acting out in various unpleasant ways. Little Lexy seemed outwardly unaware of the changes, but she frequently wet her bed after biweekly visits to dad. So the split had been a mess, as they often are; "But at least I got the house," as Gloria put it.

"Which leads to us," I said after the movie.

"Are we an 'us'?" she asked.

"Well, in a way," I replied. "And this is date number three. I've been counting. It's not hard to count to three."

She gave me a look that I couldn't interpret. Then she kissed me. It was one of those wonderful, sexy, older-woman kisses.

I responded in an obvious physical way.

"Slow down," she told me. "Wait until we get home."

Ah, such sweet words! John Keats wrote poetry about the joys of the romantic chase, about the perfection of a romance where the love never gets to the point of sex.

Bold Lover, never, never canst thou kiss,
Though winning near the goal—yet, do not grieve;
She cannot fade, though thou hast not thy bliss,
For ever wilt thou love, and she be fair!

But that was almost two hundred years ago. The world had spun around many times since, and I preferred the promise of "Wait until we get home" to the yearning of unrequited love.

We got home about ten, and Gloria paid off the babysitter along with a ten-buck bonus. The girl left abruptly, giving me a nasty look as she went out the door. Perhaps she suspected what was to follow. Perhaps she was jealous that an attractive older woman like Gloria had snapped up a potential stud such as myself.

The children were asleep, or so Gloria announced after checking upstairs. Then she offered me a Scotch, since there was no other alcohol in the house. I smiled a yes, then had to deal with confusing questions about rocks and water. Nonetheless, the drink she created hit my throat with a bitter, burning sensation that tingled from my hair to my knees. It also left me coughing, so I surreptitiously poured it on a small potted palm plant. I could almost see the plant shrivel as the Scotch hit the roots.

"Let me go change into something a bit more comfortable," Gloria said after finishing her drink.

I seemed to remember this line from an old black-and-white movie, but it still sent my blood racing. "Something a bit more comfortable"—wasn't that a euphemism for something sexy and revealing? And if Gloria was changing into something sexy, what should I do? I considered this problem for a second, then quickly took off my socks and stuck them in my pockets. I had learned my sock lesson with Shauna, and had vowed never again to be caught with nothing on but my socks.

Then I looked at myself in the hall mirror and decided to unbutton my shirt to reveal a bit of my non-hairy chest. I figured this would give me a manly, I'm-ready-for-sex look. I tried to get the same look on my face, but I wasn't sure that the effort was a success.

"Making faces in the mirror?" Gloria asked when she came downstairs. She was dressed in a very large, very cuddly bathrobe that may—or may not!—have anything underneath.

"Oh, no, not really," I said.

"Maybe you'd like another Scotch?" she asked.

"Oh, no, no. I'm fine."

"Then let's go watch a movie. The kids are asleep and the night is ours."

Another line from a forties film! Thank goodness for all those old films I used to watch with Maggie; now the subtle clues were beginning to make sense.

We got to the family room and Gloria popped a DVD of *The English Patient* into the machine, then grabbed a blanket off one chair and came back towards the couch. I was watching her every move, still trying to figure out if she was wearing anything under the bathrobe.

"So you decided not to wait for *me* to unbutton your shirt," she said, laughing.

"Well, I, uh, got you started."

"You know, with this blanket and the bathrobe, I think I'm going to get quite warm. Can you think of anything I could do to fix that, Alan?"

"Well, uh, you could, like, take off your bathrobe."

She laughed at me, as I deserved. I made a point of not using "like" like that when I spoke to Gloria so she wouldn't think I was a kid. But now I was talking just like a kid. On the other hand, maybe that's what she wanted.

"You are a bit naughty, you know."

"I try," I sighed.

With that, she opened the robe and tossed it over to one side.

Beneath the robe, Gloria was not naked—she was better than naked. She was in lingerie!

I don't think women my age know the power of lingerie. In my somewhat limited experience with girls in various states of undress, their bras and panties tended to be utilitarian, which is to say, dull. The bras and panties were white or beige cotton and rarely transparent or lacy; they did their basic job of supporting or padding or shielding various parts without suggesting that anything too enticing might lie beneath.

But not lingerie. Lingerie is smooth and lacy and suggestive and enticing.

Gloria stood before me in a silken black teddy with just a touch of lace at the bodice.

"You like?" Gloria asked.

I responded with a dropped jaw and an inarticulate moan.

In a second, Gloria had covered us both with the blanket and snuggled in beside me. We began kissing as she unbuttoned my shirt. I tried to remember Maggie's old instructions on how to deal with this moment in the process of seduction. Was the rule *Do not grope, manhandle, or squeeze*? Or was the rule *Follow the woman's lead*?

I decided that any woman unbuttoning my shirt was inviting me to explore both the lingerie and what lay beneath it.

In only a few minutes, Gloria had managed to remove all of my clothing while hardly breaking lip contact. Again, the mark of an experienced woman. My blood was racing and my mind was busy trying to think of what to do next. When does the guy put on a condom? Was this the moment? Should I ask her first? Why hadn't I practised putting on a condom so I'd know how to do it?

All these questions were zooming through my mind when the phone rang.

"Let it ring," I begged.

"It'll wake the kids," she said, suddenly practical. I think older women can do that—switch instantly from the romantic to the practical. But would she switch back again?

Gloria reached over to a side table and picked up the phone on its third ring. Something was spoken on the other end of the line, and my wonderful, sensual Gloria suddenly became tense and angry.

"Why are you calling?" she snapped.

Again there were some words spoken at the other end, but those I couldn't hear. The only words that reached my ears were from Gloria, so the other part of the conversation was just in my imagination.

"Who says that anybody is here?"

Again some garbled words came through the receiver.

"Okay, so maybe I am with somebody right now. What difference does that make to you?" Gloria snapped. "I can see who I want, when I want. We're separated, Geoff. You understand the word? I could spell it for you if that would help."

There was a pause while Geoff explained that he didn't need help with spelling.

"Don't threaten me, you jerk. If you even try to get into this house, I'm calling 9–1-1. You hear that, 9–1-1."

The garbled voice at the other end was louder and seemed angrier.

Gloria was getting angrier, too. "I'm not going to listen to any more of your threats. I'm serious. You come anywhere near here and my guy Alan will take that knife of yours and stick it . . ." I won't continue, since the conversation was getting increasingly profane. At the end, Gloria swore at him and slammed down the phone.

"Sorry," she said. "He always was a jealous bastard."

I took her in my arms, trying to comfort her as best I could. Part of me enjoyed comforting a beautiful woman dressed only in lingerie and hoped that it might be the prelude to a night of passionate love.

But another part of me was busy reconstructing the other half of the phone conversation. There were certain elements—jealousy, a knife, a threat—that were unsettling, to say the least. Where did the ex-husband live? Did he still have a key to Gloria's house? Would he, while we were making out, sneak into the house with his knife and try to use it on me or Gloria?

"Alan, I'm afraid I've kind of spoiled the mood," she said.

I kissed her tear-stained cheeks. "I still think you're wonderful," I said.

"Let me see if I can bring the mood back," she said, scrooching down on the couch.

Oh, this is good, I thought to myself. Older women know how to restore the mood, how bring a man back. Gloria was doing just that, and quite successfully, when I heard a noise somewhere in the house.

The husband, I thought. *With a knife.*

I tensed up and shrivelled up at the same time.

"Alan, what's the matter?" Gloria asked.

"I . . . I heard something."

We both listened, but there was no more sound. On TV, there was a steamy sex scene between Ralph Fiennes and Kristin Scott Thomas; on the couch, there was a potentially steamy sex scene going on between Gloria and me.

Then I heard the noise again . . . footsteps. Yes, there were definitely footsteps in the house. I was about to say something, about to overcome my fear and actually whisper a warning, when the door to the family room flew open.

"Yiii!" I screamed.

"Mommy!" screamed a child.

There was a pause. Gloria lifted her head and looked, as I did, towards the door.

It was Little Lexy, standing with her brother in the doorway. "My tummy hurts!" she cried.

Gloria sat up. The two children just stared at us.

"Why was your head in Alan's lap?" demanded the little girl.

Gloria thought quickly. "Mommy lost a contact lens," she said. This explanation seemed pretty bogus to me, but seemed to satisfy Lexy. Young Brad, however, looked at us with a weary, cynical expression. No seven year old should ever have such a world-weary look on his face.

"I need med'cine," said Lexy, holding her painful stomach for added effect.

"Of course you do, dear," Gloria told her. "Let's just go up to the bathroom and get you something."

Gloria got up and put on her bathrobe, neatly covering me up with a blanket in the process. Then she dutifully led her two children up the stairs, keeping one eye half closed as if the missing contact lens were causing her distress.

I was alone. The steamy love scene on the TV screen was finished, and now we were back in the North African desert. The not-so-steamy love scene on the couch was in pause mode.

Unfortunately, there was an ongoing problem. Even if Gloria decided to have sex with me here on the couch, there was no way I was physically capable. I looked under the blanket and shook my head in despair. I was shrivelled up by fear of discovery and general confusion. *This is not going well*, I told myself.

When Gloria returned, I had to do better. *Think erotic thoughts,* I told myself. I tried to think of Gloria in her lingerie, but that image morphed into one of her construction-worker husband holding a knife. So I thought about a girl in my women's studies course, and then about a girl I'd seen on the bus, and then about Maggie. But each of these images got confused with Gloria's ex-husband, and the kids, and the desperate situation I was now facing. Blood was racing through my head, through my body, pulsing everywhere—except *down there*.

Just when I thought that my situation couldn't get worse, there was a knock on the front door. "Gloria, open up!"

I panicked. I confess that now, because I have lived to tell the tale. I just panicked. A naked man is in no position to take on an angry ex-husband. Quickly, almost instantly, I had my clothes back on. By the time the ex-husband pounded on the door for a second time, I was putting on my socks. By the time he pounded for a third time, I was out in the kitchen, quietly opening the back door.

I stepped out into the cold night air. I was in the backyard, hiding between the garage and a small climber set. From inside the house, I could hear the sound of angry voices—Gloria and her ex—voices full of accusations and denial, anger and threats. Finally

Gloria said something like "I'm calling the police" and the husband went stomping off; the front door slammed as he left.

I was shivering, from cold or fear or both. At last I heard a car motor start up, and then the screech of tires as—I hoped—the ex-husband drove off in a rage.

When the fear died down, I realized I had a choice. I could go back into the house, wait until the children were asleep, and then try to pick up our paused sex scene where we had left off. I could pray that the intervening time would let my body recover, would let Gloria mellow out, and would give us a slim chance at restoring the mood. I could do that. I could risk another phone call, another discovery, another almost-confrontation with the ex-husband. I could be brave, bold, daring, and romantic.

Or I could slink away into the night. I could leave my jacket behind, tie up the laces on my shoes, and just slink away into the night.

May the good Lord forgive me for my cowardice!

11

Dysfunctional Thoughts

ERECTILE DYSFUNCTION! I woke up the next day thinking not about Gloria, not about the ex-husband, and not about slinking into the night. I thought about my penis.

My body had totally let me down. It had failed me in my moment of need!

If that isn't erectile dysfunction, I don't know what is. I checked the web just to be sure, but the verdict was clear. "Erectile dysfunction: the inability to obtain and/or maintain an erection sufficient for sexual activity." That was it.

Of course, age eighteen-almost-nineteen is a bit young for ED, but such cases are not unheard of. "Although erectile dysfunction is more common in men older than sixty-five, it can occur at any age. An occasional episode of erectile dysfunction happens to most males at one time or another. In fact, it's usually nothing to worry about." Ha! That's easy for the Mayo Clinic website to say, but when you're at the other end of a case of ED, as it were, it is not a trifling matter.

I had been impotent, to use that old-fashioned word. I had run the bases and was ready to run for home, but suddenly my knees (okay, not my knees, but let me go with the metaphor) collapsed beneath me. *Impotens*, to be without power, without strength, without virility. That was me. I had failed the challenge—the challenge of sex with an older women, the challenge of her threatening husband, the challenge of real life!

I was a wimp, a miserable, cowardly, impotent wimp.

So just as I was approaching midterms, I collapsed into a pit of despondency. Yes, I was powering up my vocabulary, but my more crucial parts just weren't working. Perhaps I should just give up on women and become a monk. Perhaps I should abandon any hope for sex and take a vow of chastity. Since I already suffered from ED, I really had nothing to lose.

So I emailed Maggie. I told her that my fling with an older woman had come to a crashing halt. I even told her the story of that fateful night, omitting my ED problem, of course. Unfortunately, she gave me no sympathy.

> To: amacklin@BU.edu
> From: maggiemac@sl.edu
> Serves you right, Al. You bring that poor woman into physical danger, then go hide when the husband arrives. That was not a class act, Mr. Macklin. No sense calling her again, you blew your chance. If there were a pill for courage, I'd recommend it to you, or maybe you can get some phony wizard to give you a medal, à la Wizard of Oz. In the meanwhile, might as well stay celibate.
>
> Incidentally, I've decided to take that ski invitation for Christmas. I might make a fool of myself, but I've done that once or twice before, and this guy really is quite attractive. If you're going to play around with older women, I guess that gives me permission, right?

If anything could push me lower still, Maggie's email did the trick. Why? We had gone out for a year, fooled around, but never actually had sex. We liked each other, we enjoyed each other's company, we were friends . . . but somehow it stopped there. Maggie knew it and I knew it. Prime time versus afternoon soaps—simple as that.

So why was I so upset that she was going off on a ski holiday with some guy? After all, I emailed her about my various adventures and misadventures, surely she should have the same rights. Fair is fair, isn't it? All's fair in love and war, isn't it?

Actually, no. In war, there are the Geneva Conventions. They stop an army from torturing its opponents or starving its prisoners of war or massacring civilians. So war has rules. What are the rules for romance, anyhow?

"Deep thoughts?" Kirk asked.

"Semi-deep," I replied. "Maybe shallow-end-of-the-pool thoughts."

"Deep enough," he replied, sitting down on my bed. He had to push aside my plush-toy hamster to do so.

I was sitting at my computer, trying to hammer together a three-thousand-word essay on "Bette Davis as a Feminist Avatar in the 1940s." It was actually a paper for my film class, but I figured that some of the material might work for women's studies as well. Two birds with one stone, you might say. The most impressive part of my essay so far was the word *avatar,* which meant 1) an incarnation of a god in human form; and 2) an embodiment (as of a concept or philosophy) in a being, often a person. Any essay with the word *avatar* has to be worth at least a B. Now I just needed another twenty-nine hundred words or so to finish it up.

"Al, I've been worried about you lately," Kirk said. "You don't seem to be your usual self."

"I've got three major essays due in the next week," I told him.

He shook his head. "That's not it. You could knock off a major essay before breakfast if you felt like it. What's the matter? Has it got something to do with that Gloria person you were seeing?"

I flipped around in my chair and looked at him. I guess Kirk was the only person at school who knew me well enough to see through my lies.

"Yeah, well, kind of."

"You fall for her?"

"No, nothing like that," I sighed. "It just didn't work out, that's all."

"That's all?" he asked.

"Yeah, that. And I found out I had a certain medical condition."

Now Kirk seemed almost shocked, and it took me a second to read his mind.

"No, it's not an STD or AIDS," I told him. "Nothing like that. Just a . . . a condition."

Kirk sighed, perhaps relieved that I hadn't picked up something contagious. After all, if my toothbrush had touched his toothbrush . . . well, you never know.

"You see a doctor?" Kirk asked.

"No, not exactly," I replied. I wasn't going to admit that I'd only done Internet diagnosis.

"Maybe you should hop over to the clinic," he suggested. "They were pretty good when I had that stomach flu."

"Yeah, maybe," I said. "But I'm kind of hoping the problem will go away by itself."

That sounded pretty lame. Maybe I should actually go to the clinic and tell some doctor about my ED. It would be embarrassing, of course, but maybe the doc would write me a prescription for Viagra or some other miracle drug.

"Well, good luck," Kirk said, and surely I could use some of that. "But I've got an idea that might perk you up a little. Why not come out to our ranch over Christmas? You've probably never been to a real working ranch before, and you might find it interesting.

"A ranch? Like with cows?"

"Steers," he corrected. "The house is quite big and my family is kind of interested in meeting you. You could do a stopover on your plane ticket, stay a couple days, then go on to your parents' place."

"Would I, like, have to go to church?"

"No pressure, Al. If you want to join us on Christmas day, fine. If you want to stay at the house and watch TV, that's fine, too."

"Really?"

"Yeah, really. Besides, my girlfriend and my sister, Pug, both want to meet you."

I raised my eyebrows at that. It was hard to imagine any woman wanting to meet me in my . . . condition. Anyhow, I told Kirk I'd consider the offer.

When I stopped to think about it, two weeks with my parents seemed like a very long time indeed. They had already talked to me about visiting Aunt Linda's family Christmas weekend, a plan that might be interesting if playing with five-year-old twin cousins was your idea of a good time. Maggie was going skiing, so she wouldn't be around, and my other friends were busy making plans that might or might not bring them back home. I might be spending most of the two-week vacation alone, with nothing to do and think about my . . . condition. Maybe a little time in Alberta wouldn't be a bad thing. A ranch might be interesting. Maybe they'd teach me to ride a horse or wrangle a steer or whatever people do on ranches. Surely John Keats wouldn't have turned down the chance to take a ranching vacation, if there were such things two hundred years ago.

"By the way, Kirk, how late does that clinic stay open?"

12

Nobody Messes with Pug

I DON'T THINK that medical professionals should be allowed to laugh at patients. After all, it's tough enough to go into a doctor's cubicle, knowing that anybody could be listening in, and have to whisper that you have ED. A doctor should take something like that seriously, and not just laugh at your condition.

What's worse was that the doctor only asked me a couple of questions, took a quick look down below and then said there was nothing wrong with me! What did he know? He didn't give me a referral to a specialist or a prescription for Viagra. Instead, he ignored my whole problem. "I have a hunch your penis will work just fine next time," the doctor said. Was that supposed to be encouraging? As far as I was concerned, there might never be a next time.

So I was not particularly cheerful on the brief, early-morning flight to Calgary. While I was considering a malpractice suit, Kirk was busy reading an airline magazine. I had two weeks off from studying and papers, so I should have been cheerful and relaxed. But I kept dwelling on my . . . problem. I had never before realized that I was a guy who got hung up on just one thing. *Monomania*—that's the word. Like Ahab with his whale in *Moby Dick,* I was Alan with my own miniature whale. Oh, even the metaphor was enough to make me cringe.

We got down to the luggage carousel and were met by Kirk's family. His father, Mr. Chamberlain, was a tall, distinguished-looking man who, strangely, was wearing a cowboy hat. I took this as a local custom. His mother, Mrs. Chamberlain ("Call me Jan") was a short woman dressed in denim with sequins sewn on for some sparkle. Finally, there was Kirk's sister, Pug.

"Why Pug?" I had asked him on the plane.

"Don't know," he replied. "She's always been Pug. Something about the fact that she's short and her nose is too small. A pug nose, you know?"

"Does she have a real name?"

"Who cares," Kirk said curtly.

It looked as if brother-sister relations were no better in born-again families than in most others.

"You must be Alan," said Mrs. Chamberlain, smiling brightly.

"Nice to meet you," added Mr. Chamberlain, giving my hand one of those killer handshakes. Kirk should have warned me about that.

"Hi," added Pug, looking at me shyly.

"You must be Pug," I said.

"Patti," she said, smiling. "I'm trying to get over the Pug thing."

I stood corrected. In fact, Pug was not that short nor was her nose that tiny. From what I could see, she was a pretty decent-looking teenager, a miniature version of her handsome brother. Like her mother, Patti wore jeans and cowboy boots. More than that I couldn't tell from the heavy ski jacket she wore to ward off the winter. In Alberta, the temperature can reach minus forty, the only place on the thermometer where Celsius and Fahrenheit equal the same bitter cold.

"Where's Kathy?" Kirk asked.

"At the church, dear," said Mrs. Chamberlain. "They're getting ready for the Christmas pageant. She'll meet us at the house."

Kirk frowned, obviously not too pleased with this. I guess in a born-again relationship the church always came first.

We left the airport in one of the family vehicles, this one a Cadillac Escalade. That should have been my first clue. For some reason, I had assumed Kirk was a poor kid from one of those struggling farm families you always hear about on the news. I'd assumed that Kirk's family had no more money than mine did. But when we reached the Chamberlain ranch, I realized my assumptions were dead wrong.

His dad pulled up to an elaborate entrance gate, pressed a button on the dash, and the wrought-iron slowly pulled back so we could enter the grounds. Then we drove and drove, for another ten minutes, until I could spot a house sitting on a gentle rise in the land. In fact, it was far more than a house—it was a complex. The house was just the most prominent building in the group. Trailing behind it were barns and garages and equipment sheds and other outbuildings; the whole complex would fill two city blocks.

"Here's the spread," announced Kirk's dad.

"Welcome to the ranch, Alan," echoed Kirk's mom.

I looked out at land stretching in all directions as far as my eyes could see. "Just how big is the spread?" I whispered to Kirk.

"Just under thirty thousand acres," he replied nonchalantly. "Dad transferred some to Uncle John."

I don't know much about farms and ranches, but it seemed to me that thirty thousand acres was in the category of "real big." The house was a rambling, three-storey, fake-French chateau. There were, I learned later, six bedrooms, eight bathrooms, and various special-purpose rooms—the video room, the wine cellar, the cigar room, the memorabilia room, and more.

My awe at the house extended to the girl who greeted us—the much anticipated Kathy.

Kirk's girlfriend resembled a supermodel. She had lustrous dark hair, big brown eyes, perfect eyebrows, perfect teeth, perfect complexion, and perfect breasts of a size that would rival Gloria's. She could have been strutting on a catwalk, modelling fashions in Milan, but instead was finishing up at the Christian high school in the nearest town. She was, in that old-fashioned word, breathtaking.

"Oh my!" I said when I saw her. The words just fell out of my mouth. Of all the girls with whom one might take the pledge, Kathy certainly had to be the most magnificent. I tried to imagine "waiting," but the pain was enough to make me wince.

At that moment, Kirk did not wait. He ran forward to kiss this goddess, hold her tight, and then swing her right off her feet.

"All right, you two, that's enough," Mr. Chamberlain said sternly.

Kirk and Kathy split apart, and for a second I looked at them both, as a couple. They were a perfect match: hair, teeth, complexion, bodies, sex appeal. If ever there were a match made in heaven, this was it.

"Kath, this is my roommate, Alan," Kirk said.

I was speechless. I put out my hand and got a handshake almost as muscular as that delivered by Kirk's dad. Perhaps Alberta is a province of *hearty* handshakes.

We spent the afternoon touring the ranch. I suspect this was an excuse for Kirk and Kathy to spend some time with each other, but I kept my mouth shut. Instead, I did a walkabout with Mr. Chamberlain and Patti. Mr. Chamberlain would give me some straight information, then Patti would give me a little twist on what he said.

Mr. Chamberlain: "We've got about ten thousand head here. Good mid-size operation."

Patti: "The place stinks from all the steer crap. But you get used to it."

Mr. Chamberlain: "This here's the computer room. The boys here keep track of all the animals, all the feed, all the farming. Everything's run through this server with a backup over here, and I don't understand a damn thing about it. A man can't run his own farm anymore."

Patti: "Dad can't handle computers. If a thing doesn't go moo, he's afraid of it."

Mr. Chamberlain had every reason to be proud of his ranch, which was probably enormous even by Alberta standards. Patti, of course, didn't take seriously either her family's ranch or their obvious wealth. She was, I hate to say, your basic snotty rich kid: lots of attitude and not much appreciation.

That night we sat down for dinner. Before meeting the Chamberlains, I would have expected some overcooked meat and bland potatoes. Now I wasn't surprised by the gourmet extravaganza that arrived in front of me: vichyssoise (that's creamy potato soup, I found out), Châteaubriand (a thick cut of beef tenderloin), and even a glass of wine (an Italian red called Montalcino) for those of us who were of drinking age. There was exactly one glass of wine per person since the Chamberlains had a whole set of ethics about alcohol. In fact, the Chamberlain family had a pretty comprehensive set of ethics, vaguely based on their fundamentalist religious beliefs, which I learned about through the evening.

The family also had its habits. One of them was this: after dinner, the men would "withdraw" to the billiards room while the "ladies" helped the housekeeper with cleanup. This routine struck me as pretty archaic, but I was in no position to question.

So we three men headed down to the basement-level billiards room, one so large it had both a billiards table and a pool table. Since billiards is a bit complicated for beginners, Mr. Chamberlain suggested a game of pool. Kirk went over to rack the balls while his father opened a little cabinet in the wall. Mr. Chamberlain then filled three glasses with single-malt Scotch and pulled three cigars from a large humidor.

"Can't play pool without a cigar," said Mr. Chamberlain, handing me a cigar and a glass.

"I . . . uh, don't smoke," I said. As far as I knew, neither did Kirk.

"Cigars aren't smoking," Mr. Chamberlain explained. "Smoking is a sign of weakness, a sign of sinfulness. A good cigar . . . well, that's one of God's gifts to man."

I nodded my head. While I have considerable knowledge of weakness, I've always been a bit fuzzy on the concept of sin. Of cigars I knew nothing at all. In the black-and-white films of the 1940s, only bad guys smoked cigars. Now they seemed to be a popular habit.

Before the pool game began, we went through various cigar rituals: a toast with the Scotch, the cutting of the cigar, the lighting, the smoking.

"No, no, don't suck on it," Mr. Chamberlain said.

His words came too late. A plume of acrid smoke entered my mouth and literally took over my nose. I coughed. My nose stung. I coughed again. If I had impressed anyone with my level of sophistication over dinner, that impression had now gone up in smoke.

"Just pull with your cheeks," Kirk told me. "You just want a little bit of the smoke."

I took another drink of the Scotch, which didn't seem nearly as bitter as my first taste of the stuff at Gloria's. Then I tried a gentle pull on the cigar, and managed to hold in the smoke without dissolving into a coughing fit.

"You'll get the hang of it, boy," Mr. Chamberlain said, clapping me on the back. The force was almost enough to make me swallow my cigar.

We played pool for a good half hour. I was no match for either of the Chamberlains, but I was also hobbled by the awkward cigar in my mouth and the effects of the drink. Kirk and his father seemed quite at home with this; indeed, they *were* at home. I felt I had entered into the inner sanctum of the family.

Our talk over the pool game was mostly *guy*: sports, cars, politics. Mr. Chamberlain only occasionally lapsed into talk of sin and wickedness, then would pull back so as not to offend his heathen guest. It was at the end of our pool game, when the cigars were "ashed," that the talk moved elsewhere.

"You ever shoot a gun, there, Alan?"

"No, sir," I replied. In truth, I had never even touched a gun.

"That's a shame," said Mr. Chamberlain. "A man's got to be able to hold his liquor, smoke a cigar, and shoot a gun. That's what my father told me and what I tell Kirk, here, though I'm not sure he's always paying attention."

"As much attention as it's worth," Kirk mumbled.

"Anyhow, let me show you my collection before we go up and join the women."

Kirk sighed. "The arsenal."

Mr. Chamberlain ignored his son. He went over to an indentation in the wall, then punched some numbers into a touchpad. Silently, the wall opened into another small room—about the size of my bedroom at home—but this one was lined entirely with guns.

"My dad was a collector," Mr. Chamberlain began as we entered the room. "Of course, in those days a man had to actually *use* a gun. Used to have lots of problems out here with coyotes and bears, and you want to use the right gun for the right critter. Sometimes you might want a .303, like this one here." He handed me a gun that weighed a good twenty pounds. "Or this .22, probably from the mid-1860s; doesn't shoot that straight, but look at the tooling. Now up there I've got a couple old blunderbusses, and over there a few more modern rifles . . ."

The historical arms tour went on. I had never seen so many working guns in my entire life—there must have been two- or three-hundred of them. They ranged from beautiful historical rifles to modern automatics, from handguns to almost machine guns. They were, Mr. Chamberlain pointed out, all legally registered, all safely locked up in the "arsenal."

"But they're here, just in case . . ." he concluded.

"In case of what?" I asked.

Mr. Chamberlain gave me a look of disbelief. "Well, in case they're needed. We still have animals to deal with here, and you can't stop every intruder at the gate, and there's always the chance of rebellion."

"Right," Kirk said, "we've had so much rebellion lately."

His father ignored the remark. "A man's got a right, a *duty*, to protect his property and his loved ones," he said, laying the extra emphasis on duty. "I mean, I don't worry about Kirk, here, because he can look after himself. But if I ever catch a boy messing around with my little Pug, well . . ." Mr. Chamberlain looked over the rows of neatly stored guns, perhaps trying to pick out the most lethal weapon.

Kirk filled the awkward moment of silence. "Dad, isn't it time to go upstairs?"

"Right," his father agreed. "Up we go."

Kirk and I exchanged a look, largely of sympathy. I think everyone our age knows that aspects of our parents are a little off, a little eccentric, perhaps a little crazy. This gunroom was Mr. Chamberlain's madness, and his son's embarrassment.

We rejoined the three women, who were busy watching some home remodelling show on television.

"Did he take you to the arsenal?" Patti whispered. We were in the kitchen on a mission to get seconds of dessert.

I nodded.

"Tell you about the possible rebellion?"

I nodded again.

"Did he give you the line about protecting me—'nobody messes with my Pug?'"

She did a good imitation of her dad's voice. I smiled.

Patti shook her head. "Sometimes I think he's mental."

I tried to be noncommittal on that. Mr. Chamberlain seemed very much in his right mind when he was talking about his guns and what he might do with them. Besides, I make it a habit not to argue with older people, even my father, even if they are seriously deluded. What's the point? After the age of forty, older people can't change that much—they're fossilized.

The family finished the decorating show, watched some program on VisionTV, and then Mrs. Chamberlain declared it was time for bed. Tomorrow was the day before Christmas and there was so much to do.

Kathy pulled herself away from Kirk, then got in her car and headed for home. The rest of us headed up to our bedrooms on the second floor. Each bedroom had a label on the door naming it after an English county. My room was the Dorset, actually a small suite that had a bedroom, a sitting room, and its own bathroom. The sitting room even had a small library, mostly filled with Reader's Digest condensed books and religious texts. But there was a hardbound book called *The Great Romantic Poets* with a copyright date of 1915.

That's the book I was reading, sitting up in the bed, when I heard a little tap on my door. A second later, before I could say anything, the knob turned and Pug stepped into the bedroom.

"Alan, can I ask you a question?" she whispered.

"Well, I guess," I replied.

"Do you think I'm pretty?"

13

One Problem Resolved

I HAVE NOT RECEIVED much wisdom from my father over the years, but I have learned one thing: when my mother says, "Do I look alright, dear?" the correct answer is always, "Yes, you look lovely." To offer any qualifications on this blanket approval is a mistake. To suggest that a lock of hair is out of place or the makeup is a little bit too heavy is to encourage, at best, many minutes of bathroom primping or, at worst, emotional meltdown.

So in answer to the question, I might have told Pug that she was cute, or that her pink bathrobe was adorable, or that her smile was dynamite—since all those things were true—but to change the adjective might lead to problems. So I remembered the lesson from my father.

"I think you are very pretty," I said.

"You're not just saying that?" she said.

"No, I mean it," I told her.

And actually I did mean it. Pug was not beautiful, like Kathy; she was not sensuous, like Gloria; but she was definitely pretty. She had a cute nose, pretty blue eyes, and short dark hair with blonde tints. She reminded me a little of Reese Witherspoon.

"Guys tell me I have a real nice bod," Pug said, untying her bathrobe. In a second, the robe was on the floor and Pug stood in front of me dressed in a thin white T-shirt. The fabric was see-through, so much so that I could tell Pug was wearing nothing underneath.

I gulped. "Yes, yes, you do," I agreed.

She came over to the bed and sat down right beside me. Pug was on top of the covers, I was down beneath a sheet, a blanket, and a duvet, so there were still several layers of cloth between us. My eyes, however, were not fully under my control. I kept telling them to focus on Pug's face, to pay attention to her eyes or her hair, but they kept on working their way down. She really was quite perfect, in her own cute way.

"I knew you liked me," Pug said. "I could tell by the way you were looking at me at dinner."

I didn't recall ever looking at Pug during dinner, but this was a poor time to offer a correction. "Of course I like you," I said.

"Do you think I'm hot?"

"Yes, definitely hot," I told her. "But there's this problem." Now I was squirming under the covers.

"Don't listen to my father," she said, pushing one breast into my shoulder. "He talks big, but he'd never do anything. And he doesn't have any idea what I do. I mean, I've been hooking up since I was fifteen. If dad was serious about protecting me, he'd have shot at least a couple of boys by now."

I find it difficult to think straight with a breast pressed against me. It's just hard to form a rational argument, to keep the mind under control in a situation like that.

"There's also your brother," I managed to say. "He's my roommate, maybe my best friend, and there are things you just don't do."

"Like sleep with his sister?" Pug asked.

She had pulled back the covers and was climbing into bed with me.

"Like . . . yeah," I said.

"But my brother doesn't have to know," Pug said, pushing up right beside me. "If you don't tell him, then I won't tell him. It can just be our little secret." She flipped off my reading light as if to emphasize the secrecy.

By now, her mouth was right at my neck and I could feel her hot breath on my skin. I still had the book in one hand, but soon it was flying to the floor.

Did Pug kiss me or did I kiss her? I'm not sure exactly who moved first, but in no time our lips were locked together, our tongues dancing with each other. *This is good,* I said to myself. *If nobody knows . . .*

But then I remembered my problem. I pulled my lips away from her and sat up a little to get back some self-control.

"Patti, I can't do this," I said.

"Why not?" she whispered. "I'm on the pill."

"Because . . . because it's not right, and . . . and because of my problem."

"What problem?" she asked, pulling herself back. "You're not gay, are you?"

"No, not that, it's just . . ." How does a guy admit that he's suffering from ED?

"I . . . uh. . . uh." Why am I always so inarticulate at moments like this?

"I don't feel any problem down here," Pug whispered.

I felt her hand touch me and realized the most amazing thing—she was right. I didn't have a problem. My penis was working just fine! I was cured!

In a second, she had dived under the covers. I leaned back on my pillow and enjoyed the sensations coming from down below. Whatever else Pug had learned at her fundamentalist school, she had certainly mastered one skill.

"Oh my, I think—"

But before anything else could happen, there was knock at the door. A loud knock.

Pug stopped. I froze. This was a truly awkward moment.

"Uh, yeah," I said, my voice cracking just slightly.

The door opened and Kirk stuck his head in.

"Al, you asleep?"

"Not exactly," I replied.

"Well, I've got to talk to you about something. Come down to the billiards room and we'll play a few more rounds."

"Give me a couple minutes," I said. "I'll be there."

The door closed. The little sliver of light from the hall disappeared, but not before I noticed Pug's pink bathrobe in a little puddle on the floor. Had Kirk seen that? No, the room would have been too dark. Had he seen the double shape under my covers? No, not possible. Besides, Kirk was too virtuous to possibly imagine . . .

I pulled back the covers. "We've got to stop," I said.

"I heard," Pug replied. "My brother is such a pain."

Pug hopped out of bed and grabbed her bathrobe. I hopped out of bed and tried to figure some way to deal with my *new* problem. How do you make a penis deflate?

"We've got to finish this," Pug whispered to me. "Tomorrow. It's Christmas Eve. I'll be your elf."

"Uh-huh," I said.

"And, Al," she added, "you'll be my first."

I looked up, though I could barely see her in the dark bedroom. "I thought you'd hooked up with a few guys."

"That's just hooking up," she said. "I want you for my first real sex." Then she went noiselessly out into the hall and closed the door.

I suppose I should have been honoured. Pug had chosen me to be her first real sexual partner. And wasn't sex what I'd been looking for all these years? I mean, the situation should have been perfect . . . except it wasn't.

I thought of Kirk waiting for me downstairs, wondering what was holding me up, but now I had a new problem. I was standing there in a T-shirt and boxer shorts with my penis pointed at the door. I thought about the obvious solution, but that would take too long. So I tried to talk reasonably with the problem.

"Down," I whispered furiously. "Get down!"

No response. I still had an erection that was quite painful and extremely embarrassing. It was time for drastic action. I walked over to the sink, turned on the cold-water faucet, and ran the stream over my penis.

"Ooooah!" I cried, or something to that effect. The freezing water was painful, but effective.

Quickly I threw on one of the fluffy bathrobes in the closet, then walked down to the basement. Kirk had already racked the balls.

"Took you a while," he said.

"I had to freshen up," I replied. Another forties movie line, but I think I was the wrong gender to use it.

Kirk handed me my glass and then looked me right in the eye. "Al, we've got a problem."

I squirmed. I tried to look away. I tried to stay cool and calm and collected, but none of this was working. Kirk had a disconcerting stare at the best of times, and this was *not* the best of times. "What problem?"

"My sister," he said. He seemed to be spitting out the words.

"Your . . . uh, sister . . . uh, Pug." Was I turning red in the face? Was I somehow giving away my guilt?

Kirk shook his head and looked away. I took that second to take a breath.

"Pug is out of control," Kirk declared. "My dad and I were just talking about it."

"Just now?" I asked.

"Well, for the last little while. There are things going on at that school over there . . ."

"Ah, the school," I said, breathing even more deeply. "Might be a bad crowd, even at a small Christian school." I sounded like a high school guidance counsellor.

"I don't think it's the crowd," Kirk replied. "I think it's Pug. In the last year or so, she's gone wild about guys. There have been rumours."

"Not good rumours?" I said.

"No, not good rumours," Kirk agreed. "Even my dad has heard them. So I guess that was one of the reasons I asked you to come out here. My dad and I were thinking that maybe you . . . well, you're a decent guy, Al. We can trust you. Some of the guys at school, well, they might take advantage of Pug. But, you—"

I said nothing. How could I say anything?

"—anyhow, it looks like Pug likes you. Maybe you noticed over dinner, how she was always looking at you. It must be the attraction of the older, experienced man."

I blushed. I think I really blushed. "Must be," I said.

"So we were thinking, maybe you'd be willing to play along. I mean, my sister is just a kid, really, so if she hooked up with you it would keep her from getting in trouble with some of the guys at school."

I had a hunch that "hooked up" meant different things for Pug and for Kirk. I just gave my friend a look.

"I mean, you don't have to do anything," Kirk said. "Just be nice to her, pretend you like her, and then set up some kind of long-distance romance. It'll keep her happy and preoccupied, and by the summer, you can drop her and maybe this crazy stage will have passed."

"You're kidding," I said.

"Al, I know it's a lot to ask," Kirk concluded, "but it would really help us out. I mean, you're the only person we can trust for something like this."

"Oh my," I sighed, and nodded my head.

14

The Most Frustrating Christmas Pageant Ever

I PRAYED THAT NIGHT. Maybe I was moved by all the religious books on the shelves, or maybe it was all the talk about sin and righteousness, but I actually prayed. It feels good, really, getting down on your knees and asking Somebody Else to solve your problems. It takes a little weight off the shoulders and gives you some perspective on the world.

The only person we can trust. That was the most galling phrase. They trusted me! My best friend and his family were delivering their delightful Pug into my hands, trusting me not to do exactly what my body so desperately wanted to do.

In any other circumstance, in any other situation, I could have taken advantage of my good fortune. I had a more-than-willing girl, two more days of opportunity, and a house so large that surely there were rooms we could use. I even had her family encouraging me to "be nice" to her.

But no. *How low are you?* I asked myself. *How low will you sink just to get laid?* There are limits, after all. There are moral standards. All is not fair in love and war. And if I should be weak, if I should give in, how could I ever justify it to Kirk, or his family, or Maggie, or even my own nagging conscience?

So my mind was resolved. I would be like Odysseus lashed to the mast of his ship in order to resist the temptations of the Sirens. I would be strong. I would be resolute. Of course, Odysseus had a bunch of ropes holding him back, not to mention a shipful of sailors whose lives were at stake, but I still liked the analogy. At least I got one thing from my Humanities class. I could picture

Pug as a Siren and me, roped to the mast, resisting her song. Glorious. Heroic. Admirable.

Then there was real life.

The day before Christmas, we all gathered in the kitchen to have breakfast together. When Mr. Chamberlain asked us to bow our heads in a prayer, Pug ran her bare foot up my leg. When Mrs. Chamberlain was telling us about the upcoming Christmas pageant, Pug extended her leg beneath the table so that her toes could play with my crotch. When Kirk said how helpful it would be if I would look after Pug for the day ahead, she gave me the most devilish grin imaginable.

Stay lashed to the mast, I told myself.

The Christmas celebration at their church was an all-day extravaganza that included everyone in the family. The older members would sing, or organize, or help out; and Pug had a role in the pageant. When we assembled in the living room, she appeared already dressed in her costume.

"How do you like me?" she asked.

In truth, she was the sexiest angel I had ever seen, or could possibly imagine.

Mr. Chamberlain decided that we should travel in a car convoy from the ranch to the church. The two parents would drive in the Escalade, Kirk would drive his own vehicle, a little SUV, and I would take Pug in the pickup truck. The plan, of course, was to give Pug and me some time alone together.

I still find it difficult to remember the drive. Let me say, metaphorically, that this Odysseus was lashed to the steering wheel while the Siren beside him did her best to destroy his willpower. Fortunately we reached the church before my resolution crumbled altogether.

I'm told that the average Christmas pageant lasts only an hour or so, but the Christmas celebration at the Chamberlains' church seemed to go on for most of the day. It began, not long after we arrived, with some full-throated Christmas carols in the church basement. I saw that Kathy was playing the piano, seated beside some guy who was turning the pages of the music for her. Obviously she was both beautiful and talented. When the crowd was exhausted, the adult choir did a few songs, and then the children's choir raised their voices. This brought us to lunch, served by the church ladies—every bit as good as Kirk had told me—and then to preparations for the pageant itself.

I was assigned various duties: hanging lights, wiring the star of Bethlehem, and guarding the llamas. I realize that there are no llamas in the Christmas story, indeed, there were no llamas at all in the Middle East at the time, but they were as close as the congregation could come to camels in the middle of an Alberta winter. My guarding of the llamas was fairly simple: make sure the animals didn't run away, make sure they didn't bite or spit at the children, and make sure the children didn't bite or spit at the llamas. I managed this job splendidly. Odysseus could not have done it better.

At two o'clock, the pageant began. Mostly the event seemed to be about animals, small children, and adults with video cameras. There were times when I thought the pastor might ask everyone to do the whole thing over again, just so the parents could improve their camera angles.

I can report that the children were excellent in their roles, the animals reasonably good, as animal actors go—except for the donkey, which resisted any effort to make it move. And the Herald Angel, in her tight-fitting outfit, was a tremendous hit among the male members of the audience.

"Go thou, wise men, to Bethlehem where this day is born the Christ child," Pug intoned as the Herald Angel. "Go see the infant Jesus. Though he was born in a humble stable, and sleeps now in a manger, yet he is the Son of God."

The three young wise men responded enthusiastically and led the llamas off to the final scene of the pageant. As they made their way, the Herald Angel saw me in the audience and delivered both a smile and wink.

Ah me, I sighed. Somehow I had to resist not just Pug, but the Herald Angel. Already I was sliding into lustful thoughts. All the

Christmas carols seemed filled with double entendres, all this celebration of salvation and rebirth seemed as nothing in comparison to my lust.

"Was I good?" the Herald Angel asked when the pageant was finished.

"Incredible," I said.

"I could wear this outfit tonight," she suggested. "Would you prefer an angel or an elf?"

"An angel seems a bit sacrilegious."

"Then I'm your elf, Alan. Let me tell you what this elf can do."

I must admit that Pug, the elf, had a tremendous imagination for someone who had never actually had sex. Indeed, as she whispered her ideas, I found myself responding in a very unChristmaslike way.

Be strong, I told myself. *Be resolute*.

Both strength and resolution would improve if I had a plan. I considered various options. I could pretend to be gay, but my obvious physical attraction made that a bit implausible. I could fake some dreadful disease, perhaps throwing up after dinner in a most unattractive way, but that would only delay the issue. I could make myself so crude and obnoxious that she might find me totally disgusting. On the other hand, Pug might just find that even more attractive. Given her whispered suggestions to me, perhaps that's just what she had in mind. I could invent an alternative girl—a Gloria—to whom I had pledged to be faithful. But I suspected that Pug could quickly overcome that defence.

So what did that leave? It left a Christmas miracle, or a second Christmas miracle, if you count the first.

Christmas Eve dinner was a marathon of sexual teasing. I suspect Pug enjoyed the semi-public display, perhaps finding the possibility of discovery something that added to the excitement. There were ten of us at the table—the senior Chamberlains, Pug and me, and six relatives of various shapes and ages whose names I tried very hard to remember. Kirk and Kathy were over at Kathy's house, doing the night before Christmas with her family after promising to have Christmas dinner at the Chamberlain house.

If Kirk had been there, perhaps Pug would not have been so outrageous. As it was, she enjoyed flirting with being discovered. It was bad enough to have her rubbing her foot up and down my leg throughout the meal, but still worse were the rubs she'd give me in between.

In a situation like that, almost every word becomes a double entendre. All those ordinarily mundane aspects of Christmas dinner—from "Would you like some breast or some leg?" to "This meat is so juicy"—take on second meanings. If I missed any of these, Pug would give me a little squeeze or a faster rub.

I had to distract myself. *Think about high school geography,* I told myself. *Think about the craters on the moon. Think about anything but sex.*

All this was made worse by the fond smiles I kept getting from Mr. and Mrs. Chamberlain. They obviously approved of Pug's whispers and smiles, thinking that these were early signs of a slowly blooming romance. Little did they know of what was going on beneath the table, or in their daughter's imagination.

"Alan, you seem a bit warm," Mrs. Chamberlain said at one point. "Should I turn down the thermostat?"

"Oh, no," I sighed, probably turning more red in the face. "It's just all the food."

"Alan's always hot," Pug added, squeezing me beneath the table. "Isn't that right?"

"Well, sometimes hotter than others," I said.

"We have an ice cream cake for dessert," Mrs. Chamberlain said. "That should cool you off."

"Ice cream . . . yes, that would be good."

Pug leaned in and whispered another suggestion for the ice cream. Then she sat back and smiled at me, her face looking quite angelic with blue eyes, big cheeks, and one perfect dimple. Ah, the irony.

When Mr. Chamberlain announced that the "men" were retiring for Scotch and cigars, somehow I managed to pull myself together so I could stand up without embarrassment. I smiled politely at Mrs. Chamberlain and the aunts, then managed to leave the room with some dignity, though perhaps not walking quite as I usually do.

I believe I smoked the cigar with greater aplomb this second night, though without much enjoyment. The Scotch, on the other hand, was starting to grow on me. I've never quite understood alcoholism, though this stuff was beginning to make sense of it. For a second, I pictured myself as a skid row bum, ruined by his addiction to single malt. Then I caught sight of the arsenal and the picture shifted to me lying in a ditch, a large bullet hole where my stomach had once been.

"Good to see you getting on with Pug," Mr. Chamberlain said to me as he racked up the balls. He turned to one of the uncles and explained, "We're hoping Al will win my little Pug's heart and keep the kid out of trouble."

"The boy's doing all right," replied one uncle. "She was snuggling up against him all through dinner."

"And what was all that whispering about, Al?" asked the second uncle. "You looked a bit riled up."

"Oh, Pug likes to make jokes," I lied.

"Thought she was going to eat your ear, boy," said uncle number one. Then he turned to Mr. Chamberlain. "That girl doesn't need a boyfriend," he said, "she needs a chastity belt."

Mr. Chamberlain looked up from the pool table. "Well, if it all works out, Al here is going to be that chastity belt."

The two uncles laughed. Mr. Chamberlain frowned. I drained my glass in a single gulp.

Be strong, I told myself. *Be resolute.*

I had just lost a game of pool to uncle number one, who was a pretty good player, when we heard the garage door open and close. There was a brief discussion of who might have driven in, but since there was no obvious answer all the men decided to go upstairs to see.

We had just reached the kitchen and rejoined the women when the door to the garage wing opened. It was Kirk. He had a terrible look on his face, a look that combined all the worst features of anger, loss, and despair.

For a moment there was simply silence in the room. The obvious question was hanging in the air, and Kirk said nothing. We waited. The clock ticked. And finally one of the uncles broke the silence. "What is it, boy?" he asked.

Kirk stared at all of us, one at a time, and then told the whole story in two words.

"That bitch!"

15

True Love Doesn't Always Wait

KIRK'S OUTBURST REFERRED, of course, to the world's most perfect girlfriend and almost-fiancée, Kathy. My roommate did not immediately explain just what issue had come up between them, and that wasn't the most pressing issue since his use of a five-letter expletive violated the family code of ethics. Despite Kirk's obvious distress, his mom took the moment to remind him of proper language in the Chamberlain house.

Perhaps for that reason, Kirk was not very interested in filling in the family on details. Nor was he interested in the remains of our turkey dinner, or his father's general comments to the effect that "She's just a girl," or his sister's observation, "I never trusted that Kathy—she was too good to be true." He was sunk into a despair so profound that it made his little dust-up with Kathy in September seem like a lover's tiff.

"Al, let's play pool," was all he said.

I hesitated for a moment, and then I realized that my redeemer had, in fact, arrived. I shot Pug a look of reluctant acquiescence, a look that told her how awful it would be to postpone our Christmas festivities, but that the emotional needs of my friend had to come first.

When Kirk and I got to the billiards room, it was soon clear that the real attraction was not the pool, or my companionship, but the single malt in Mr. Chamberlain's liquor cabinet.

We dealt with Kirk's crisis the way men do—by pretending to ignore it. Under the male code, men talk about nothing emotional or personally important until we have exhausted a goodly supply of liquor and all the safe conversational topics: cars, sports, and politics. Since I know very little about cars, sports, or politics, our conversation was focused on the game in front of us and the drinks in our hands. It took two hours for Kirk to get back to the events that made him look like Oedipus after the bad news.

"It was the page turner," he mumbled.

"Nine ball, corner pocket," I replied and then took my shot. I missed. "The what?"

"The page turner," Kirk repeated. He chalked his cue. "At the Christmas pageant, didn't you see that geek turning pages while Kathy played? I should have been able to spot it right then." There was a pause while he eyed the table. "Four ball, side."

He sank the ball. Kirk was very good at this game, and he got better when he was angry.

"So it was another guy?" I asked.

"Yeah. Three ball, bank." He sank that, too.

"She told you?"

"I said the page-turner guy was getting pretty close up on the piano bench. I mean, I wasn't doing a big jealous thing, just observing." He paused. "Six ball, combination."

"Then she told you."

The six ball went in. "Yeah. Had to confess the whole thing. Thank you, Kathy, I really needed all that on Christmas Eve. That's what I should have said."

"What did you say?"

"Nothing," he replied. "I choked." He looked up at me for just a second. "You know, Al, I loved that girl. I trusted her." But that was enough sincerity. Then it was back to the game. "Two ball, corner."

"Nice shot."

"Thanks."

"Eight ball, corner." He sank it. "Game. More Scotch."

So the story emerged in bits and pieces, over many hours, while we drained most of the bottle. This left me a bit tipsy, since I'm really not used to drinking, but Kirk was too angry to show any effects.

While it may be possible for true love to wait, exactly how long it will wait seems pretty variable. It appears that Kathy had been reasonably faithful until some time after Halloween, when the evil influence of lust and the advances of an available young man took their toll. I was certain, though Kirk was not, that Kathy made some effort to resist both the lust and the young man. Perhaps it was the proximity that did it: the two of them side by side at the piano bench. Perhaps it was just the influence of fate. Nonetheless, the otherwise perfect Kathy gave in to temptation. I actually had some sympathy for Kathy, especially because I myself was no stranger to the sin of lust and know how hard it is to resist temptation.

Unlike Kirk last fall, Kathy had made no confession via telephone, nor did she send a contrite letter begging for forgiveness. Instead she let the illicit passion grow. I suspect, though Kirk would disagree, that Kathy had some intention of breaking it off. I suspect, though Kirk would deny this, that she felt quite guilty and conflicted. Indeed, she might well have kept the whole thing hidden had not Kirk become suspicious. When confronted, Kathy blurted out the truth. Did Kirk really want to hear that truth? Probably not, but Kathy offered up her affair in a tearful confession on Christmas Eve. Happy holidays.

Kirk reacted like a gored bull moose. He had been insulted, betrayed, and lied to by a scheming woman. "A Jezebel," he declared, and I vowed to look up who Jezebel might have been. I suspected she was not a very nice person.

I didn't try to speak sensibly about any of this. A man in the midst of jealous rage does not want to hear sensible thoughts: he wants to swear, blaspheme, and otherwise spew it all out.

And then the guy gets worn out. After five hours of venting, Kirk was finished—knocked out by anger and sadness and injustice and Scotch.

"Bitch," he said. It came out a bit slurred: bissh.

"Not worth your time," I agreed.

"Here's my Christmas present. Here's what I got." He reached into his pocket and pulled out a girl's ring, obviously Kathy's ring: "True Love Waits" was inscribed on the silver band.

"Ironic," I said as he threw the ring on the pool table. "Might as well throw yours away, too."

"Yeah," he said, tossing it at Kathy's ring.

In that moment, as the two rings collided, I had a sudden flash of insight. Kirk's grief might solve my problem.

When I got up to my room, there was a note on the bed written in a young girl's curly script. "Your Christmas elf couldn't wait all night. Tomorrow I'll be your Christmas present." There were the usual number of *x*'s and *o*'s, followed by Pug's signature.

A few hours before, such a note would have brought more panic. But now I had a plan. On Christmas morning I would be ready. I would be as wily as ancient Odysseus.

Unfortunately, I had to put my plan into effect a bit earlier than I had thought—at five A.M. to be precise. I was lying in bed, asleep, when I heard my name.

"Alan," whispered the voice. "It's Christmas!"

I opened my eyes and saw nothing, but felt a weight on my bed. Bleary and hungover, I tried to wake up. At the same time, Pug turned on the little lamp beside the bed.

There she was, my present, wearing little more than a bright red bow.

"Oh my," is all I could say. I sat up in bed so I could get a better look.

"Do you like the outfit?" Pug asked.

"It's . . . uh, very attractive," I coughed out.

"I brought us candy canes," she said, handing one to me. Then she began licking hers in a way that can only be described as lascivious.

Oh no, I said to myself, *I'm giving in. I'm losing my resolve.* I had to act immediately and be decisive and follow my plan.

"Patti," I said, using her real name to add gravity to the situation. "You are the most beautiful, most irresistible girl I've ever met. I mean, being here with you is like a dream come true. You're a fantasy, a delightful Christmas fantasy."

She smiled as I waxed poetic. It was all quite true, really, except for the irresistible part. I kept hoping that Patti would be quite resistible, or else I'd have a lot of explaining to do.

Be strong, I told myself. *Be resolute.*

Pug climbed under the covers with me. Her hand traced its way down my chest . . . and lower. The best-laid plans of Alan Macklin's brain might soon be lost if this kept up.

"I'm ready," she whispered. "And so are you."

Be strong. Be resolute.

"But, Patti," I went on, "you're so much more than a fantasy to me. I realize that I've only known you for a couple of days, but I feel that I've known you all my life."

Groan. I'm sure that line bubbled up from one of those 1940s movies, but I figured I should heavily lay on the romance. Pug, I knew, wasn't terrifically interested in romance, so somehow I had to re-aim her lust in the direction of love.

"High school boys can't appreciate someone like you, Patti. You're so much beyond their level."

"I am?"

"Oh, you are," I said, my voice full of sincerity. "You know how special you are to me. I mean, that first kiss yesterday was . . . I can't tell you . . . it was like I'd been waiting my whole life to meet you."

"Really?" she asked, wide-eyed.

"Not the word of a lie," I said, lying quite handily. "And now, well, you can feel how ready I am for you, how much I want to make love to you."

"Yeah, me too. Can we, like, do it?"

"But Patti," I croaked. *Be strong, be resolute*, I told myself. *Think of the Chamberlains, your roommate, your sacred honour.* "We can't."

"We can't? Why not?"

"Because I'm in love with you," I whispered. "Because I want this moment, this first sexual moment, to be as special and as wonderful as it can be."

"Well, so?"

I saved my best line for last. "Because true love waits."

"Ohmygod!" she shrieked. "Have you taken the pledge?"

"Of course," I lied. "I thought you would have, too."

"Yeah, but it didn't mean anything. They made all the girls in school take the pledge. Look how long it stopped Kathy from screwing around on my brother."

"But that's not the point," I told her. "The pledge means we have a real loving commitment, that we're not just two horny people hopping into bed."

"But I'm okay with that," she said eagerly. "I mean, I'm horny and we're already in bed."

"I want more than that for us," I sighed. I hoped my sigh was full of romantic languor. "So I'm going to give you your Christmas gift a little early. I'm sorry, I didn't have time to wrap it."

I reached into the drawer in the bed table and pulled out the girl's "True Love Waits" ring that Kirk had thrown in disgust on the pool table. I held it in my hand for a second, and then whispered, "This is for you, my love," as I put it on her fourth finger.

"Ohmygod," she repeated. Either Pug was quite moved or she was at a loss for words.

"And there's one for me, too," I went on, picking up Kirk's old ring. "True Love Waits," I sighed.

Pug seemed to think about all this for a while. Then she asked the question that had been plaguing Kirk earlier on. "Yeah, but how long does it wait?"

"Till the summer," I said. Surely I'd come up with another plan by the summer. Or maybe by then I wouldn't need a plan at all. "Then we can have hot, sweaty sex."

"Hot . . . sweaty," she repeated.

"It will be wonderful. It'll be worth waiting for."

"Oh, that will be so cool" she sighed. "I mean, like, so hot. Hot and sweaty." With that promise, I think I had won her over.

"Thank you," I said. I felt my performance had been pretty spectacular too, all things considered.

"But I've got a question," Pug said, pushing herself into my arm. "I can see waiting for sex, but does that mean we have to wait for everything? I mean, your elf wants to make you happy."

"Oh, I think there are lots of ways we can make each other happy."

16

Happy Holidays

CHRISTMAS MORNING WAS a bit stressful at the Chamberlain home. We gathered around the tree with a variety of emotions and expressions on our faces. Kirk, of course, was extremely unhappy, verging on morose, given the events of the day before. By noon, he avoided going to church by claiming illness, both physical and spiritual. He went back to bed.

Mr. and Mrs. Chamberlain soon noticed the TLW ring on Pug's finger, and gave me wonderful smiles of approval. Much as they were distressed about Kirk and his failed relationship, they were heartened by the pledge Pug and I had taken.

Pug and I were looking a bit conspiratorial that morning. The reason was simple: my answer to her last question was a no. True love does not have to wait for everything. In fact, true love can accommodate all sorts of very satisfying things up to, but not including, intercourse itself.

I had not, technically, had sex with Pug. There had been many activities in my bedroom that morning, some of them even a bit noisy, but I had stayed true to my commitment. I had been strong and resolute. I had kept my sacred honour intact. I had respected the trust of my roommate and his family . . . mostly.

My only regret was that my virginity, like hers, was still intact.

I spent two more days at the Chamberlain house before flying home. I kept busy by consoling Kirk, playing pool with his father and uncles, and stealing a few wild moments with Pug. Now that Pug and I both wore our rings, the family was content that their daughter was being looked after. As for me, I found that looking after Pug was a burden that came mixed with certain benefits, as the phrase goes. When I flew home, there was a moment of real emotion as I said goodbye to her at the airport. But then I flew back to my real life.

When I got back to my house I decided to use my dad's computer to email Maggie and see how her Christmas vacation in Vermont had gone. I knew that Maggie wasn't much of a skier, but I suspected that the skiing was just a pretense to lure her to a remote and romantic winter hideaway. Somebody with far more money than I had was putting on the moves.

From: amacklin@BU.edu
To: maggiemac@sl.edu
Much enjoyed Christmas ;-) Kirk's born-again family turned out to be far more interesting than I could ever have imagined. And you'd be proud of me. I managed to fight off the lustful intentions of Kirk's younger sister with a resolve that impressed even me. Let me know when you get back to your dorm and I'll tell you more.

BTW: How was skiing in Vermont? Were you able to schuss your way down the hill, or were there unfortunate moments along the way?

I thought that was a pretty impressive email. I liked the phrase "lustful intentions," which sounded like the title of a Victorian porn novel. I also thought the word *schuss* was quite impressive, and I really will look it up some day.

My surprise was that Maggie emailed back right away.

To: amacklin@BU.edu
From: maggiemac@sl.edu
No schussing. All moments were unfortunate. I am not at the dorm but back here at home, about ten blocks from your house. Come see me. I'm miserable.

I borrowed the family car to drive over. *I look good*, I said to myself as I checked my appearance in the mirror. Perhaps clean living pays off with a clearer complexion; perhaps my stoic resolve was being rewarded with a more attractive physical presence. Perhaps, I thought, Maggie will notice the difference.

But the difference to be noticed was in Maggie.

"What happened to your hair?" I asked. Maggie has always had frizzy flaming red hair, lots of it, usually piled or pinned in various shapes. But today her hair looked like she had chopped it short with a pair of scissors—herself—when she was half-drunk.

"I'm tired of hair," she said.

"How can you be tired of hair?"

"Hair is bourgeois. It is part of a whole industry that seeks to trivialize and sexualize women. I'm tired of that, too."

Poor Maggie sounded so tough, yet so forlorn. She was acting like a feminist intellectual, but that was only on the surface. Underneath, she was hurting. I could see it in her eyes.

"Do I look that bad?" came her small voice.

"Nah," I lied. "It was just the shock when I first came in. I kind of like your hair short." I thought it was a pretty convincing lie. In fact, Maggie looked halfway between Andre Agassi after a bad day at the barber's and Wynona Ryder in *Girl, Interrupted*.

"I look bad," she went on. "It's how I feel. I'm pathetic."

Then the most extraordinary thing happened. Maggie started to cry. I've known Maggie for ten years, gone out with her for an entire year of high school, but I'd never seen her cry before. Even when she'd fall flat on her face playing soccer, or when she got dumped, Maggie didn't cry. But now a tear was gathering in the corner of her right eye, and slowly dripping down beside her nose. Then a tear appeared in her left eye, and another in her right, and finally Maggie sobbed.

"I'm an idiot!" she cried.

"Oh Maggie, Maggie," I said, wrapping my arms around her. I could feel her body shaking as the tears fell. She felt skinnier than I remembered, and she was trembling as the sobs came out.

"It was awful," she wailed. "Christmas was awful."

That afternoon I found out how awful it had been. Maggie had gone off to a ski chalet in New Hampshire, with a senior named Pinney. I assumed that was his last name, since no other name came out in the story. Maggie was thinking about romance and candlelit dinners after days of invigorating skiing on the easy slopes of Killington. Pinney was thinking about sex. He provided just enough romance, candlelight, and skiing to move quickly to the sex.

"He got me drunk the first day," Maggie said. "Can you imagine that? This dumb little nineteen-year-old broad wasn't even smart enough to watch her liquor."

"And then?"

She looked at me, hard, her eyes still brimming with tears, and couldn't speak. The words for what happened just couldn't come out, only tears.

I held her as she cried. Poor Maggie. I had never seen her so weak, so vulnerable.

I must have held her for ten minutes before she could say a word, and then the words were still punctuated with tears and anger. "All last year, Al, I wouldn't let you do it. You. A nice guy. A guy who really cares about me, and I wouldn't let you."

I remembered that quite well.

"And then I slept with him. I'm such an idiot."

"It's okay, Maggie."

"No, it's not okay. It'll never be okay."

I got sad along with Maggie, and then I got angry. I reacted like a jealous father, or maybe a jealous boyfriend, ready to go off and beat this guy to a pulp. Of course, I had never beaten anyone, much less to a pulp, but that's what came immediately to mind. We are simple creatures, we humans, with simple emotions in some primitive part of our brains.

"I made him fly me home," she told me.

"I'm glad you're here with me," I said.

"Me, too," she replied, snuggling against me. "You make me feel safe."

"Thank you," I said.

"You are so decent, Al. I mean, you want to get laid just like all the other guys, but at least you're decent about it."

Maybe not always so decent, I thought.

"I'm giving up on men," Maggie announced.

"Really? Like, forever?"

"Forever. Men are pigs and idiots. All of them."

"All of us?"

"Present company excepted," Maggie said.

Ah, Maggie, I thought. It felt like we'd spent our whole lives together, from the days when we played soccer—her a skinny little redhead and me a stumbling and uncoordinated kid. And then high school, through the dating-advisor stage, to the dating stage, to the girlfriend-but-no-benefits stage. And now this.

"Now what about your Christmas?" Maggie asked, breaking into my thoughts. "And what's the story with this ring?"

I told my story well, I thought, emphasizing the funny parts and leaving out the activities of Christmas morning. My story made Maggie laugh, and she needed to laugh. Her life had gotten far too serious over Christmas.

During the rest of the holiday, more details kept bubbling up from both Maggie and me, though I still kept the most sensitive aspects—make that, the most indecent aspects—to myself. By New Year's, we had shared all the stories and characters of our first semester. When we went to our friend Scrooge's New Year's party, Maggie and I kissed at midnight. It was a wonderful, serious kiss that reminded me of everything I had ever felt for Maggie.

"Hey, can I get another one of those?" I asked her.

"Don't get carried away," she said.

"Why not?" I asked her. "What's wrong with getting carried away?"

"Distance."

I knew the answer to that one. "Distance makes the heart grow fonder."

"Pretty conventional line, Al," Maggie sighed. "But in the real world, distance and absence are the same thing."

17

The Great Unfolding of the World

Kirk and I returned to campus with new dedication to our studies. My roommate was developing quite an obsession with sin and the fall of man. I was developing a real fondness for the movies of John Wayne. Admittedly, there was an intellectual gulf between these two interests, but there was a surprising amount in common. Kirk would tell me about Eve, Jezebel, and Satan. I would tell him about Jane Russell and Mae West and the evil Nazis in Germany that were heroically defeated, film after film, by the mighty efforts of John Wayne and the troops. Kirk would tell me that the movies of John Wayne showed a Manichean world view. I would nod my head and vow to look up *Manichean.*

Like Maggie, Kirk had decided to give up on the opposite sex. I couldn't say I blamed him. Once a man is betrayed by the world's most perfect girlfriend, how can he trust any woman? Perfidy, thy name is Kathy!

Got to look up *perfidy,* too.

Because the Chamberlain family had banned the Internet, all I heard from Pug came via letters and the occasional phone call. She was obviously having trouble with the concept of true love waiting. Her sexual frustration might even have been affecting her spelling, judging from the letters she sent.

> *Al,*
> *I get so hot thinking about you. This wating thing is driving me crazy. When can you get back here so we can do it? There are so many guys at school who just want to*

hook up, but I tell them I'm devoated to you. I'm counting the days to the summer. Come back to me, lover, and we can have some swetty spring sex.

Patti xxooxx

I did not share these letters with Kirk, who would have found their contents disturbing. When Patti really got into her fantasies, her girlish handwriting and creative spelling seemed at odds with the pornographic content. Thank goodness her missives didn't come in by email—her material would have been deleted by the college's web server.

I was obviously under some pressure to fly back to the ranch for Spring Break, but I feared that my strength and resolve would break down with even a few days of Pug's temptations. I kept dodging that issue, wondering if I could claim heavy studies as an excuse to stay in the dorm.

It was my old friend Scrooge who gave me a better way out.

To: amacklin@BU.edu
From: scroogedude@um.org
Got an idea to bring you out of the sexual wasteland. A couple guys here are planning a Spring Break trip down to Puerto Vallarta. That's in Mexico, in case you're geographically challenged. There will be free margaritas, cheap cervezas, and maybe excellente señoritas. What do you think, amigo? And what about that roommate of yours? Or maybe somebody else from your dorm. The more guys we get, the cheaper the trip.

So I emailed back:

To: scroogedude@um.org
From: amacklin@BU.edu
Familiar with Mexico. Looking forward to margaritas and señoritas. Will work on finances and get back to you.

There was some back-and-forth emailing about the trip. It turned out that the cost would come in at nine hundred dollars, or less if I found some other guys, and that included all the margaritas I could drink. Since I had never had a margarita, that sounded quite enticing. What's more, if we were doing the spring break in Puerto Vallarta, I couldn't very well go off to see Pug in the middle of Alberta. This trip would preserve her virginity and perhaps give me a chance, in Mexico, to lose my own.

For a fleeting moment, I thought my parents might be disappointed if I didn't come home, but my father didn't sound the least bit upset when I brought it up. "Your mom and I were thinking of a little holiday just by ourselves," he said, suggesting that the house would be mostly empty should I fly home. What's more, Maggie's Spring Break didn't coincide with mine. She'd be home the week before me and back in school by the time I got to town.

So my decision was simple. My problem was the nine hundred dollars. Now this is not a large sum of money in universal terms. There are people out there, driving around in Rollses and Bentleys, for whom nine hundred dollars might be a tip for the car park boy. But for those of us surviving on a Macklin family scholarship—and who were fully reminded of that with each weekly phone call—then nine hundred dollars is a considerable sum. I needed some very creative way to come up with that kind of money. So I went to the university website and took the link to "grants and bursaries."

There it was: Continuation of Studies grant. Just complete a form, submit a transcript of your marks, write a pleading letter, and the committee could give you up to a thousand dollars for books or expenses. Surely Puerto Vallarta would fall in the category of expenses, but I decided "books" would look better on the form. I wrote an excellent letter about expenses being higher than anticipated, and my poor parents stretching every nickel to pay my tuition. I suspect neither Keats nor Shelley could have written a better begging letter.

Since Scrooge wanted some deposit money quickly, I decided to take my application letter right to the Dean's Office where I was asked to sit and wait for a few minutes. I opened a copy of *Burrard Life*, a publication about our school that had obviously been sanitized for alumni reading. I had never, on campus, seen as many handsome, smiling undergraduates as I found on the first twenty pages of the magazine.

I was midway into a piece called "New Academic Laureates on Campus" when the receptionist called my name.

"Mr. Macklin," he said, "Ms. Thayer will see you now."

I gulped. "Ms. Thayer?"

"Yes, she handles all grant applications."

Oh my. I suppose I could have backed away and started running somewhere, anywhere but here. But Gloria must already have my name and a retreat at this point would look more cowardly than . . . well, more cowardly than I had shown myself to be a few months back.

So I steeled myself and walked down the row of tiny cubicles to the one marked "G. M. Thayer." I tried to compose myself before going in. Exactly what expression should I have on my face? The last time I had seen her, I was lying naked on her couch while she put a sick child to sleep and her angry husband pounded on the door. So should I present myself with a smile, a look of apology, a look of deep sadness? I decided that a poker face would be best. Reveal nothing. Say nothing to remind her of that night.

I knocked on the door and went in.

Gloria looked up over some half-glasses. She was just as fabulous and sexy as the last time I had seen her.

"Ms. Thayer," I said. It wasn't a question, just a recognition.

"Alan," she replied, equally serious. "We meet again. What can I do for you this time?"

My mind played with that question. Perhaps I'd been listening too much to Pug and her double entendres.

"I'm . . . uh, applying for a continuation grant."

"You have the paperwork?"

"Right here," I said, handing the envelope to her.

"Just have a seat while I check through this." It was all so businesslike. Who would ever expect that this woman and I had shared a few very intimate moments? "No other scholarships?"

"No. My parents are footing the bills."

She gave me a look. Somehow the difference in our ages and stations in life, never very important before, seemed to loom between us like the Great Wall of China.

"And you need the money for . . . ?"

I cleared my throat. "Books."

She smiled. "You know, Alan, a few students come in about this time to see if we'll finance a Spring Break trip. You wouldn't be thinking about that, would you?"

"Oh, no," I lied. "I'm too broke. Besides, I have to study."

She smiled, then went back to looking at the form I'd completed. I noticed that there was now a ring on her left fourth finger. I wondered what that might mean.

"Okay, Alan. I'll send this through and email a response by the end of the week."

"Thank you," I said, rising from my chair. I turned and had reached the door to her tiny office when she stopped me.

"Alan," she said, her voice taking a new tone. "I am sorry about that night."

"You are?" I gulped.

"Yes. Of course, all that is over now. But you might be interested to know that I'm back with Geoff again."

Geoff the jerk must not be that much of a jerk, I thought. "Oh," I said.

"So it was all for the best," she told me. "Thank you. You restored my faith in myself."

"I did?"

"You did. Wait for the email and have fun over Spring Break."

So I left the Dean's Office with a considerable smile on my face. Perhaps my years of sexual frustration all had a purpose, perhaps they were part of the great unfolding of the world. Perhaps they were evidence of divine intervention or at least of a divine design to the otherwise random events of life.

Or maybe not. When the grant notice came in on Thursday, I suddenly had nine hundred and forty-five dollars to apply to Spring Break . . . and maybe to buy a book or two.

I emailed Scrooge to tell him that I was in, then sent him enough money to cover my share of the deposit. In reply, Scrooge asked again about Kirk and other guys on the floor. Apparently adding them would drop our cost by another hundred dollars. "Enough for a full night of debauchery, señor," Scrooge wrote.

So I approached my roommate that night.

"I was wondering if you might want to join me on an expedition over spring break," I began. "A week-long anthropology course."

"Could be interesting," he said. "I wasn't looking forward to going back home. Where's the course?"

"Puerto Vallarta."

"In Mexico?"

"Si, señor." I was getting as bad as Scrooge with the Spanish.

"An anthropology course?"

"An unofficial course," I explained. "A chance to study the habits and habitats of college students on vacation. You could do some direct observation of their activities, take field notes, perhaps get some personal experience to augment the fieldwork."

Kirk shook his head.

"It would tie in nicely to your study of sin and temptation," I went on. "Years from now, you could do a bunch of sermons about the evils of drink and the flesh. And while you're there, you can enjoy the sun, the surf, and some splendid relaxation."

"How much?" he asked.

"Eight hundred if you're in. Seven hundred if we find one more guy."

"You need company?" he asked.

"I always enjoy your company," I told him, since that was the truth.

Kirk gave the entire concept about thirty seconds of thought.

"Sun, surf, and drinking?"

"And a chance to observe sin from up close. At least, I hope so."

There was a pause. Kirk got one of those inward looks, the kind where he stops focusing on the world around him and begins thinking deep thoughts—about morality, the self, the soul, sin, redemption . . . whatever. Since I never have those thoughts myself, I could only speculate what went through his mind. But I did know how to wait patiently, and my patience was rewarded.

"Alan," he said at last, "count me in."

My very religious roommate sometimes managed to surprise me.

18

Two Blasts of Heat

WE ACTUALLY FOUND one more guy to join us on Spring Break—Fuji from the room beside us in the dorm. Like Kirk, it had taken Fuji all of ten seconds to make up his mind. Unlike Kirk, he brought his laptop with him for the trip and managed to annoy us by playing video games all the way.

When we finally stepped off the plane, Kirk, Fuji, and I were hit by a blast of dry heat. Mexico in March is hot, very hot. We sweltered in the customs line, then dripped while waiting for the prearranged taxi that would take us to the hotel. We were staying north of the old city, in a suburb called Nuevo Vallarta, a complex of hotels, restaurants, and marinas that was created entirely for tourists. The taxi dropped us at our hotel, one of ten virtually identical high-rise hotels that lined the Pacific shore. We called upstairs to Scrooge and found that the others, our roommates for the week, had already arrived from their various schools.

Scrooge greeted us at the door. "Alan, my man," he said affably, "and Kirk, I've heard you're one cool dude. And you must be Fuji," he added, eyeballing the computer under Fuji's arm. "Here, have a *cerveza*," he said, handing us all a beer. "*Cerveza numero uno*."

"Did you ever study Spanish?" I asked him.

"Irrelevant, Alan," Scrooge replied. "All romance languages are basically the same as English. You just add an "o" wherever it sounds good and sprinkle in a few local words like *cerveza* and *margarita*. Don't they teach you anything at BU? Now come in and meet the other guys."

There were eight of us in Scrooge's crew, six of us legally booked into two rooms at the hotel and two guys who bought air-only tickets and were basically camping out in sleeping bags on the floor. Introductions were quick. In the other room there were four buddies of Scrooge. The first was Aiden, a guy who looked quite Irish with his dark curly hair and bright eyes. He even seemed to speak with something of an Irish lilt, though he was actually born in Detroit. Beside him was Matt, a short guy whose hair kept flopping down over his eyes. Matt was an aspiring artist, he said, who got sidetracked into an art history major under pressure from his parents. Flopped on a chair was an enormous guy called Biff, short for Beefsteak or Bismark or something like that. While it is a cliché to say that very large, athletic guys are stupid as bricks, it would only be accurate to say that Biff was large, athletic, and stupid as a brick. Their last roommate was called Goofball, which must have been more accurate than his real name since that real name was never used. Goofball had the look of a man seriously brain-damaged by drug use—and he was only twenty.

Our room had the "executives," as we called ourselves: Scrooge, Kirk, Fuji, and me. Fuji got the floor, and was wise enough not to complain.

At this point, all of us—except Kirk, of course—had Mexican beers in our hands and smiles on our faces. Outside, the Pacific surf was crashing on the beach. Inside, the Killers were blasting out of a CD player that someone had brought along.

"Okay, listen up," Scrooge said, turning down the music. "Now that everybody's here, it's time to figure out what we're doing this week."

"Yes, suh!" shouted Biff.

"I am not your drill instructor, Biff, merely the organizer of this Spring Break excursion. Now, is anyone here seriously interested in Mexican art and culture?"

Silence. Not even Kirk raised his hand.

"How about Mexican music, traditional or contemporary or whatever?"

This time Kirk did raise his hand.

"That's what I figured," Scrooge sighed. "And what about the rest of you? I know that Alan here really wants to get laid."

I turned red in the face. Was it that obvious?

"Yeah, getting laid is, like, real good," Biff said, suddenly on my side.

"And getting stoned," added Goofball, who already was.

Fuji looked up from his computer. "I like to dance," he said.

"And I wouldn't mind getting drunk," Aiden threw in.

There was considerable agreement with this suggestion. As some philosopher must have said: If Spring Break isn't about getting drunk, then what's it all about?

Scrooge shook his head. "Okay, it looks like Kirk and I will be doing the cultural excursions on our own. The rest of you can spend the week as you see fit. We are open-minded, if nothing else," he said. Then he took a pause to swig on his beer.

"But there are a few rules, gentlemen. We're really packed into these hotel rooms, so don't trash up the place. And if you end up vomiting in the room, you clean it up. The maids shouldn't have to deal with your junk or your spew. Fair is fair."

There was general nodding from the group.

"Now, Alan," Scrooge went on, "this is for you just in case you manage to get lucky. We need a signal system for a little privacy in the rooms."

I had never realized just how organized Scrooge was. Still, I rather doubted that I'd be the one needing privacy.

"So, if you see a shirt hanging on the room doorknob, that means privacy for the couple inside. But privacy doesn't last forever. A gentle knock on the door, like this—tap-tap-tippity-tap—tells the couple inside that they have twenty minutes to finish up. Got that?"

"Hey, I need more than twenty minutes," Aiden whined.

Scrooge sneered at him. "Dream on, Aiden. From what I hear, twenty seconds would be about right."

"Hey—" Aiden began, but his words were drowned out by our collective laughter.

With the next round of beer, we decided to spread out over the various hotels on the Nuevo Vallarta strip to check out the bars and the girls. We'd reconvene back at our hotel—El Paradiso—just before the dinner buffet.

So Kirk and I slathered on sunscreen and ambled down the beach, heading south. Kirk was in his anthropological mode, taking note of the girls and guys at the various bars and hotels we passed. I was into a survey of the quality of the various one-dollar beers that were being served, though I'm really not that much of a beer drinker. It must have been the bargain factor. Regardless, I had decided to have a *cerveza* at each of the hotels we stopped at, so I was feeling quite cheerful—if a bit bloated—by the time we hit the El Paradiso. Kirk finally decided to join me in drinking, and ordered up the first margarita of his oh-so-sheltered life.

While we were sipping our drinks, I came to the realization that I was catholic. This was not in terms of religion, but in terms of the girls. While Kirk kept on favouring the traditional fashion-model look, I found myself more catholic in my tastes. There were thin girls, like Maggie, with small breasts and virtually no shape, whom I still found wonderfully attractive. Then there were traditionally perfect girls, the flawless swimsuit models whom Kirk preferred, who also appealed to me. Then there were the girls with fabulous style—blonde bimbo, or red-headed vamp, or dark-haired temptress, or bespectacled intellectual—and all of those girls appealed to me, too.

"I think they're all beautiful," I said to Kirk, looking around with my eyes hidden by dark sunglasses.

"You have catholic tastes," he replied.

"It really has to do with how you define beauty," I went on. "As Aristotle once said . . . actually, I can't remember what Aristotle said, because that was first term, but surely there are many *kinds* of beauty."

Kirk nodded, and we began one of our many long, and ongoing, philosophical conversations. I found that I could even keep up my end of the conversation while eyeballing the various bikini-clad girls who were running around the pool deck and up to the bar.

I was looking at a particularly curvaceous blonde and explaining to Kirk why her revealing bikini was really not as attractive as a more demure suit might have been. Kirk was responding with some quite reasoned discussion of the expression on the girl's face, and how hard it was to really appreciate a girl when her eyes are hidden behind sunglasses. I thought our discussion was at a very high level, given the general subject matter . . . and the seven beers I had had already that afternoon.

That's when I heard voices above and behind us.

"They're scoping," said one.

"What's that?" said another.

"Scoping the girls," explained the first. "It's like being a voyeur, only more adolescent."

"Oh," replied the second voice, obviously not understanding a word of the explanation.

I turned and looked up.

Staring into the sun, it was hard to see very much. There seemed to be two girls just above us, one somewhat taller and somewhat blonder than the other.

"Hello there," I yelled, smiling broadly. Seven beers do have an effect.

"Hello down below," called the shorter girl. "My friend says you're adolescent."

"Actually," I said, "I'm aspiring to be childish."

I thought that was a terrifically funny line. After seven beers, anything even vaguely amusing can seem terrifically funny. I even began to laugh at my own wit, then decided this would not do. It would not be seemly. I'm amazed how, when I'm half inebriated, words like *seemly* pop into my brain.

The shorter girl giggled; the taller one snorted in derision.

"I suspect you'll get your wish soon enough," she said.

This exchange had garnered Kirk's attention, and he now craned his neck to match mine.

"Who's your hunky friend?" the shorter one asked me.

"His name is Kirk," I told her. "He's very serious, whereas I'm very funny. Take your pick." This was not entirely true since both Kirk and I can be serious or funny, depending on the timing and subject matter. Nonetheless, I thought it was impressive that I could still use the word *whereas* in conversation.

"I'm not picky," said the shorter one.

"And that's your entire problem," hissed the taller one. Then she turned to us. "Ciao, bambini. Enjoy your drinks."

"Are we going to see you girls later?" I asked. This sudden boldness surprised even me. Then again, on Spring Break a guy can't waste any time.

"Depends," said the tall one. Her voice was bored.

"Depends on what?"

"On the Mayan gods of chance." Then she turned to the shorter one and sighed, "Freshmen," before the two of them walked off.

I brought my gaze back down to the pool level, but saw that Kirk still had his neck craned to follow the disappearing girls.

"I think we're in Paradise," Kirk said to me.

"That is the name of our hotel."

"No, did you get a look at the tall one? She's perfect. I mean, she's perfection itself. She's an angel." He sighed.

Given my previous experience with angels, I said nothing.

19

A Brief Cultural Excursion

THE MAYAN GODS OF CHANCE did not bring those two girls back into our lives that night. Instead, the gods left us at our hotel bar with a fair sprinkling of attractive girls now dressed for dinner in party clothes. These party clothes (sometimes with bikinis underneath, sometimes not) revealed a great deal of shoulder, a fair amount of midriff, and an enormous amount of leg. They were, I concluded, almost as revealing as bikinis. What they mostly revealed was a fair amount of sunburned skin. Even the girls who had dutifully gone to the tanning salon to get ready for their Spring Break trip were now reddening from the Mexican sun.

So, in fact, were we. Big Biff seemed the most burned. His light skin was now a painful pink. Kirk, for whatever reason, seemed to tan rather than burn. And I fell somewhere in between with a red nose, a painful set of shoulders, and—of all things—sunburned feet.

We were comparing burns and tans when an exceptionally good-looking blonde came walking into the bar. She was, quite literally, breathtaking.

"Mine, gentlemen," Scrooge declared.

In a flash, our leader was on his feet moving in the direction of the girl. Seconds later, he was busy chatting her up. Minutes after that, he was running his finger lovingly down the pale skin of her arm.

"How does he do that?" Kirk asked me. Some loud rock music was blaring at us, so he had to shout.

"Do what?"

"Just walk up and talk to a girl like that?"

"Alcohol helps," I said.

"So what does a guy talk about?" Kirk asked.

"You mean, you've never picked up a girl?"

"Alan, I'm going to be a minister, remember? I've only been involved with one girl in my life and I met her at school."

I nodded. "Right. Well, from my vast experience—"

"Vast?"

"Okay, my limited experience, the procedure goes like this: approach, smile, say hi or hello or *buenos noches*, ask where she's from, make a little joke about something, then tell her that something about her is particularly wonderful."

"Like what?"

"Like anything—her eyes or hair or nose ring or whatever. Just don't compliment her boobs, her butt, or her tattoos. That's considered poor form."

"Gotcha."

"You have your eye on somebody?" I asked.

"No, just wondering," Kirk replied. "This is anthropology for me, that's all."

It was not anthropology for the rest of us. Scrooge disappeared very quickly with the blonde, perhaps the first of us to use the signal system back at our room. Biff actually found two girls to feel the muscles on his arms, though their interest in the muscle that was his brain seemed limited. Aiden was trying to make moves on a pretty girl with curly hair and a bad case of shoulder sunburn. Matt was trying to hook up with a spectacularly tall girl, a girl who so towered over him that he had to crane his neck to avoid looking right at her boobs. Goofball was up dancing and had found a half dozen girls who were willing to hit the dance floor with him. Fuji was doing his robotic DDR dance, much to the delight of many girls who seemed to find it interesting.

And I wasn't doing so well. My first foray was aimed at a gorgeous streaked-blonde girl wearing an off-one-shoulder top and a short flouncy skirt. I followed my own instructions to Kirk, but the results weren't good. It's always a bad sign when you're trying to chat a girl up if she keeps scanning the room looking for some guy who might be hotter. After ten minutes I gave up and went off for another beer.

"Shot down?" Kirk asked. He actually had a notebook out and was writing in it.

"No response," I told him. "Looking for the man of her dreams, I guess."

"Going to try again?"

"Have to repair my ego first. I'd go get a beer but I'm a little wobbly on my feet." Actually, I was a lot wobbly, or staggering, as the case may be.

"I'll grab one for you," Kirk replied. "I need a refill of my Coke anyway."

I watched Kirk make his way to the bar. He was dressed, as I was, in the college-student-on-Spring-Break style: an oversized print shirt, khaki cargo pants, sandals. On Kirk, this outfit seemed to emphasize his big shoulders and muscular legs. On me, I realized, this outfit made me look gawky and skinny. Of course, Kirk worked out every day and I merely *thought* about working out, and rarely even thought about it more than once a week. That difference leads to some differences in the way bodies develop and clothes hang.

It also leads to variations in attractiveness. Three different girls came up to Kirk as he moved through the crowd and stood at the bar. Each of them made their flirtatious girl moves, and each of them was politely received and dismissed by my roommate. In the five minutes it took Kirk to get me a drink, he received more female attention than I'd gotten in the last five hours.

What is it about some guys? Kirk was not *that* handsome. Admittedly, he did have this general resemblance to Hugh Grant or Brad Pitt, but he didn't have killer dimples or an especially engaging smile. Nor did he have Scrooge's aggressive, outgoing personality. In truth, Kirk was quite shy around most people and often preferred reading a book to going out to a bar. So how could such a guy be such a chick magnet?

Irony, I said to myself. It's the principle of irony. Because Kirk wasn't interested and didn't want sex, girls naturally threw themselves at him. He had a careless attitude towards women—in contrast to my bumbling and continuing efforts at getting laid—which must have been irresistible. By not wanting them, he made the girls want him.

That, and he was better looking.

"Cheer up, Al," Kirk said, plunking down my beer. "It's only day one. In another day or two, you'll have found the girl of your dreams. There must be five thousand girls on this stretch of beach."

"Yeah, yeah," I sighed. By this time of night, the many one-dollar *cervezas* of the day were taking their toll on me. I was simply amazed at the way guys like Biff and Aiden could down beer after beer, interspersed with margaritas and topped off with tequila shooters, and still remain standing—if not particularly lucid. As for me, I simply felt exhausted and soon fell into a dreamless sleep.

We spent the next day nursing vicious hangovers, except for Kirk, who actually ran two miles down the beach and worked out in the hotel gym for half an hour. There are times when I'm ready to strangle him out of sheer envy.

That evening, Scrooge suggested that he and Kirk head downtown for an excursion—something about Mexican art, music, and culture.

"Hey, what about me?" I asked.

"There may or may not be girls, Al," Scrooge replied. "And the Mexican señoritas are off limits. You'll probably do better here at the bar."

"Yeah, but I'm interested in culture, too," I whined. "I'm an English lit major. I know about Shakespeare and Milton and Keats and Shelley. Besides, I don't feel like hanging around here and getting hungover again."

"And what about me?" Aiden piped up. "Culture is, like, my middle name."

Scrooge rolled his eyes, but the matter was decided. The four of us squeezed into a tiny Volkswagen Beetle that had had its passenger seat removed to make extra room for human cargo. Scrooge, Aiden, and Kirk crammed together on the back seat and I sat down, facing backwards, on the floor pan. Judging by the erratic acceleration and braking, dizzying turns, and the expressions on my friends' faces, it was probably just as well that I couldn't see out the front window.

We poured out of the taxi at the north end of El Centro, paid the driver a handful of pesos, and set out down the road. Shortly we were on a broad boardwalk that hugged the Pacific Ocean beach on one side and was dotted with shops, bars, and clubs on the other. Out on the water, a handful of tour boats lent their lights to the purple glow of the horizon. A few stars dotted the dark sky and a sliver of a moon had risen just over the water, its reflection rippling with the waves.

Scrooge was our tour guide. "Gentlemen, this is a cultural tour, so we begin at the Malecon, which is Spanish for boardwalk or something like that. In Mexican society, families walk the Malecon so eligible señoritas get a chance to eyeball the eligible young men of the town, and vice versa."

"Kind of like cruising," Matt volunteered.

"But with chaperones," Scrooge said, "always with the intention of marriage, and all under the watchful eyes of the Virgin of Guadalupe." He gestured towards a large church at the end of the Malecon.

"How'd you get to know so much about this?" I asked him.

"Deep study and much reading in cultural anthropology," Scrooge replied.

I shook my head. "No, really."

"My parents," Scrooge admitted. "If you go on a family vacation with two schoolteachers, you pick up a few things."

So we strolled down the Malecon, eyeballing the sunburned tourists who, like us, were in town for Spring Break, and admiring the beautiful Mexican girls—so demurely dressed—with their shy eyes and innocent smiles. It seemed like the whole city was out for a stroll—families with young children in white shirts and white dresses, groups of young teens in out-of-date T-shirts, old people with canes, and beggars wrapped in shawls and blankets.

"Are you taking notes?" I asked Kirk.

"Just mentally. Quite a difference in mating rituals."

"The Mexicans versus us?"

"Yes," he sighed. "Makes me wonder how we lost our innocence."

This conversation was getting way too profound for my hungover brain, so I went back to gazing at the ocean to our right and the sea of people to our left. We could have strolled down the entire Malecon in this way, but Kirk came to a sudden halt.

"It's her!" he shouted.

"Who?" Scrooge asked.

Kirk could barely spit out the words. "The girl from yesterday. The tall one. The perfect one." He gulped and took a breath. "She's in that bar. She's there!"

"Gentlemen, I thought this was going to be a *cultural* tour," Scrooge sighed. "But if you can't control yourselves, then Aiden and I will just have to go on by ourselves."

"Go," Kirk told them. "Go on. We'll catch up."

"Or not," I said to Scrooge, punctuating my words with a wink.

20

So Much for Culture

PEPE AND ROSA'S WAS identical to a dozen other bars that lined the eastern side of the Malecon. It was open to the Pacific on one side, with a view that took in the horizon and the ships bobbing in Banderas Bay. With its corner location, the north side of the building was also open to a side street so the patrons could watch strollers on the Malecon. At the back was the actual bar, constructed from a long piece of some kind of Mexican wood. The south side was closed by a wall in front of which the band performed—when there was a band—or a guitar duo when there wasn't. There was a small dance floor in front of the stage area, but it was unused when we arrived because the guitar duo's music didn't really inspire dancing. Compared to the blaring music coming from other places on the Malecon, Pepe and Rosa's was relatively subdued.

But that's where they were: the tall girl and her short friend from our afternoon scouting at El Paradiso.

"Isn't she fabulous?" Kirk asked.

Indeed, the tall blonde was quite fabulous if you like that tall, flawless-face, perfect-hair, I'm-so-beautiful-everywhere-I-could-model-for-*Glamour* look. Actually, I'm quite okay with that look, but I know full well that such goddesses are not interested in me.

"Yeah, sure."

"And her friend isn't bad."

The shorter girl was a bit more my level. She had smallish eyes, a nose somewhat too large, streaked hair that was probably brunette, and a probably attractive body. I say "probably attractive" because it was difficult to tell. The fashion industry has come up with revealing garments that show large amounts of flesh, but also manage to push up, push out, pull in, and otherwise redistribute that flesh.

"Not bad," I agreed.

"So how do we do this, Al? I mean, I think I'm interested, but I've never really talked to her so, well, maybe I'm just getting carried away."

"It's Spring Break, Kirk. The lust is contagious."

He shot me a nasty look, which I probably deserved. I really had no way of knowing if Kirk was feeling lust, or simply admiring the girl's physical beauty. Maybe it wasn't fair to attribute my own base motives to my roommate.

"So, look," I said, "I'll be your wingman."

"What's that?"

"It's the guy who goes after the *other girl* so his buddy can get the hottie," I explained.

"Well, I suppose."

"Fine," I told him. "So I'm your wingman, but after this you owe me one."

I took the lead, since that's the wingman's role, and walked right up to the table with the girls. I tried to look confident, which was actually much easier to do because I had so little investment in the outcome. I really was doing a favor for my roommate.

"Ah, we meet again," I said. I grabbed a seat so I could sit right beside the tall blonde. This position gave me eye contact with my target girl.

"Ah, the freshmen return," said the tall girl. "They never have heard a discouraging word."

"And the tequila keeps flowing all day," I said, to complete the song lyric. "Lovely to see you again," I said.

"Hi, guys," chirped the shorter girl. She was smiling broadly, probably quite thrilled when Kirk sat down beside her.

"Hello again," I said. "I'm Alan and this is my friend Kirk. You can call me Al, and Kirk, well, I guess you can call him, uh . . ." So much for my brilliant lines.

"Kirk," he jumped in. "Kirk Chamberlain." Then he actually reached out to shake hands. Kirk is so uncool, but somehow he makes it work.

"I'm Lacey," replied the short girl, "and this is Nicole. She's like my oldest friend." Again the big smile. I was starting to like little Lacey on the basis of her smile alone.

Nicole, however, remained an ice goddess. "So, Alan," she said, ignoring my invitation to use Al, "what inspires you to barge into our little table?"

I was ready for that one. "Curiosity, romance, and a personal fascination with girls who have butterfly tattoos on their shoulders." This was a direct reference to Lacey, who giggled at being given the attention.

This was the moment when Kirk should have said something, should have commented on Nicole's wit or her eyes or her hair, but he seemed to be choking on any kind of speech.

"Not just scoping the girls in the bar?" asked Nicole.

"You have wonderful recall," I replied. "But that was just a little afternoon silliness, and this . . . this is tonight. The sun is down, the Mayan gods of chance are at work, and they've brought us to your table at Pepe and Rosa's. Surely that's more than coincidence."

"My friend can get carried away," Kirk said, his eyes fixed on Nicole.

"Carried away!" I went on, obviously carried away by the sound of my own voice. "Kirk, look at that purple sky over the wonderful Pacific, listen to the waves crashing on the beach, smell the beautiful night air—this is like Matthew Arnold only better and warmer and more romantic!" Not bad, really. I'd managed to cover the landscape, make a literary reference, and throw in some romance. Pretty smooth.

"Are you an English major?" asked Lacey. Her pronunciation of "English" came out a little slurred, perhaps by too much tequila: *Englisshhh*.

"English poetry and women's studies," I replied. "So what do you study? I can tell you're from the East, but where? Are you Ivy,

Seven Sisters, Big Ten, Canadian, American? Exchange students? Tell us everything."

"Seven Sisters," said Nicole. "But it should be sisters with brothers, now that they've let the boys in."

"Vassar, Wellesley, Sarah Lawrence?"

"If you must know, it's Sarah Lawrence," said Nicole.

I blinked. I was about to ask if she had met Maggie, but Lacey jumped in before I could get the words out.

"I'm SUNY at Potsdam," she said. "Nobody's ever heard of that."

"We're Burrard U," Kirk added. "Equally obscure."

Kirk's line gave me a moment to think. I remembered one of Maggie's first emails to me from Sarah Lawrence, and decided to fling it at the ice queen.

"So, Nicole, are you in the production of *Lysistrata* or the Simone de Beauvoir discussion group, or are you above all that?"

The expression on Nicole's face was one of astonishment. Perhaps I had been a little too nasty.

Fortunately, a mariachi band chose that moment to start a version of *La Paloma*. Their blaring noise was enough to eliminate any conversation, so we just sat back in our chairs for the entertainment. The mariachi band had impressive costumes with silver studs and elaborate embroidery, like some Hollywood concept of a Mexican cowboy, but their music was pretty iffy. Still what they lacked in ensemble and pitch they made up for in volume. They moved from *La Paloma* to *La Malaguena* and seemed to play without a break until Kirk waved them over to our table.

"Do you know *Amor Prohibido*?" he asked the leader.

"Si, señor," came the reply.

Suddenly we were surrounded by the band. If their singing and playing had not been of the highest order on stage, it was even worse when we were in the middle of it. Still, there was a charm to the music that started to work after a while.

Both Nicole and Lacey seemed impressed, if not by the music, by the easy way Kirk had brought over the band to play for us. In fact, I was impressed too. Where did he learn to do that?

When the playing had finished, Kirk stuffed a tip into the leader's hand and the group moved off to another table. We ordered another round of drinks and the ice, as the phrase goes, had been broken.

There was a quick adjustment of chairs so I ended up in conversation with Lacey, and Kirk ended up with Nicole. As wingman, I had succeeded in my mission—hooking up my friend with his target girl. Unfortunately, this left me chatting with a half-drunk girl from upstate New York.

I learned that Lacey was a history major, wanted to teach high school to disadvantaged kids, had two brothers and one sister, drove a Volkswagen Beetle, liked the Killers and Avril Lavigne but had never heard of the Thinkertoys.

This last bit of information removed her from serious consideration, as far as I was concerned, but then the mariachi band started up again on stage and drowned out any conversation. So we talked in fits and starts all evening, the girls and I punctuating each fit and start with another drink—beer, rum, tequila, margaritas—they kept on coming. Kirk, of course, drank Pepsi.

All that time, Nicole had my roommate fixed in those big blue eyes of hers. I believe she was actually batting her eyelashes, something I'd only seen in movies, and she kept finding ways to touch Kirk on the arm or the chest. By two in the morning, while Lacey and I still sat a dignified distance apart, Nicole had virtually glued herself to my roommate. Then again, Kirk had done nothing to resist. Who knew what might have happened if Lacey hadn't broken the mood.

"Nikki," groaned Lacey. "I'm feeling just a little funny."

"You shouldn't have had that last shooter," Nicole told her.

"Yeah, but . . . well, Al was buying so how could I say no?"

"I agree, saying no is not one of your strengths," Nicole replied. "But now you're looking kind of green in the face."

Lacey giggled. "Me? Green? Can't be green. Martians are green, not me. Green, no way! No green! I'm fine."

One thing I've learned about drinking is that anyone who says "I'm fine" has had at least one drink too many. In Lacey's case, it was probably a half dozen drinks too many. When she got up to demonstrate her sobriety, she virtually fell over the Mexican man at a table behind us.

"I'm sorry, Kirk," Nicole said. "I guess we have to go." Nicole sighed and grabbed Lacey to keep her from falling over.

"We'll take you back," Kirk volunteered. "I'll flag a taxi and we'll get Lacey to the hotel."

"I'm fine," Lacey kept repeating.

Nicole looked at Kirk; he looked back. It was one of those frozen moments, when the cinematographer calls for a full-frame closeup.

"That would be wonderful," Nicole whispered.

So the four of us climbed into another Volkswagen cab without a front seat, and once again I found myself sitting on the front floor pan. Kirk was between Nicole and Lacey, his arm around Nicole's shoulders. Lacey was behind the driver so Nicole was directly in front of me. This left me staring, despite my best efforts otherwise, directly at Nicole's legs. Given the scenery, it might have been a very pleasant ride. But Lacey had a problem.

"I don't feel so good," Lacey announced.

The erratic steering of our driver had not been the best thing for her green condition. She was looking, if it were possible, greener.

A few seconds later, Lacey repeated herself with a little more emphasis. "Like, I *really* don't feel good."

"We're almost back to El Paradiso," Kirk said, reassuring her.

"I don't think . . ." Lacey went on, but did not conclude her sentence with words. Instead she leaned forward and began to vomit. Massively. Explosively. The spew hit the back of the driver's seat, then puddled down into the floor pan beside me.

"Oh dear," Nicole said.

Kirk put his arm around Lacey's shoulder to comfort her, but Lacey did not need comfort. She needed an oversized vomit bag. Her stomach was still churning with tequila, margaritas, and various unnamed shooters that were mercilessly bubbling inside her.

"Are you done yet?" Nicole asked.

"No, there's more," Lacey cried.

This time Lacey managed to get the door open so she could vomit outside the car. I was grateful for such small mercies. The floor next to me was vile enough already.

At last our taxi driver pulled off the road. He looked back at us and muttered a few phrases in Spanish that were lost on me. Only the last words had meaning.

"One hundred dollars. One hundred dollars to clean."

"You've got to be kidding," Kirk said.

"One hundred dollars, not pesos. One hundred dollars. Cash. Pay or police."

"That's highway robbery," Kirk declared.

"It was your driving that made my friend sick," Nicole added. "We won't pay a penny more than the fare."

"Then ees police!" shouted the driver. And once again we were careening down the twisting roads of Puerto Vallarta.

21

Lineup

So it transpired that four ordinary North American students ended up at a Mexican police station in the middle of an otherwise gorgeous moonlit night.

There was much shouting and gesticulating from our cab driver, with pointing at the relevant evidence, and considerable head shaking from the machine-gun-toting police officers. I'm not sure whether it was the confusing Spanish, or the prospect of dealing with the Mexican justice system, or our general embarrassment at the situation, or the fact that Lacey was still sick and threatening to do further damage at the police station . . . but we settled. Fifty dollars cash, plus the fare: total of $66.75 or the peso equivalent, which seemed astronomical.

This hit to our wallets and our pride put a damper on the romantic spirit of the evening, perhaps even more than Lacey's explosive illness. We returned to our own hotels in a different taxi (another fifteen bucks), and with a plastic bag in case Lacey should feel the urge for further cab decoration.

Scrooge and Fuji were already asleep. In seconds, so were Kirk and I. For me the evening continued through the night with dreams inspired by tequila, the Malecon, the girls, the taxi ride, and the police station. I awoke at one point in a terrible sweat, convinced that my body was covered in tequila and that I was about to be shot by a Mexican police officer who looked, in my dream, very much like Pancho Villa. In another, more pleasant dream, I was falling into the space between Lacey's breasts, fighting for breath as I dived headfirst towards her tequila-laced navel.

I mention these dreams because the second one, at least, turned out to be prophetic.

At the noon buffet, we exchanged accounts of the night before. We told the others about our evening at Pepe and Rosa's and the detour to the police station. Biff and Matt talked about their exploits at the Hotel El Paradiso. Goofball tried to remember how he ended up climbing three sets of balconies on the outside of our hotel. Fuji remained strangely silent, until we declared him "inscrutable" and forced him to tell us about an Asian girl he'd met. Scrooge and Aiden had found their own mariachi bar, said to be the best in Puerto Vallarta, and then gone on to further drinking at a place called Señor Giraldo's. This establishment, by their report, offered more drinking contests and general debauchery than any of us had encountered so far. Naturally the others were eager to join in.

"Later, gentlemen," Scrooge concluded. "We have a heavy afternoon ahead of us with eating, drinking, suntanning, and siesta-ing. Alan, is siesta-ing a verb?"

"Close enough," I told him.

"Then let's get to it!"

Most of us were exhausted that afternoon, so spent it alternately sleeping and jumping in the water at our hotel pool. These activities were accompanied by considerable slathering of suntan lotion, which, when your own supply has been used up, turned out to be very, very expensive at the hotel gift shop. The ordinary rhythms of life did not seem to apply to Spring Break, or perhaps they were turned upside down. We stayed up all night, slept through the mornings, dozed through the afternoons, and didn't become fully conscious until eight o'clock in the evening.

For most of us. Only Kirk managed to keep some semblance of normal life. He still jogged two miles down the beach and worked out in the hotel before I woke up. That afternoon by the pool, while I was mostly comatose, Kirk actually did laps! No wonder the guy hadn't an ounce of flab on his body. No wonder he had to fight off the girls with water wings and swim floats.

Kirk, of course, was appalled at the idea of Señor Giraldo's and told us, simply, that he had another plan. Naturally that plan involved me.

"I need you as wingman again," he told me mid-afternoon.

I groaned.

"Come on, Al. Lacey is a very nice girl and last night she was hanging on your every word."

"Last night she was almost dead drunk and simply trying to focus on my face," I replied. "Besides, she's not very bright. I never realized it before, but I really prefer girls who can think."

"Okay, she's not like this Maggie you keep talking about, but Maggie's not here and Lacey is. Besides, Nicole tells me that her friend is . . . what's the nice way to phrase this?"

"Easy?" I suggested.

"Well, perhaps a girl who might not resist you as much as the other women in your life."

What a great euphemism! Sometimes Kirk's verbal skills are truly dazzling.

"And, Al, the bottom line is that Nicole won't go out for dinner with me unless we go as a foursome. Lacey is her best friend and she promised to look after her. She can't just dump her to go out with me . . . and this is their last night here in PV. Al, it's my last chance."

"Last chance at what?"

"Significant conversation," Kirk replied. "You might not realize this, but Nicole was quite active in her church and she's thinking of a minor in religious studies."

"Ah, ri-ight," I said, trying not to seem too skeptical.

"Please, Al, I'll owe you."

"Big time," I concluded. "You'll owe me big time."

So that evening, while Scrooge led the rest of our group off to Señor Giraldo's for an evening of drinking and wet t-shirt contests, Kirk and I headed off for dinner with a somewhat defrosted ice goddess and her friend, Miss Projectile Vomit. The sacrifices we make for friendship!

I do have to give Kirk credit for finding a very romantic place for the girls' last dinner in Puerto Vallarta. On one of his daily jogs, he had run across a restaurant that was literally on the sands of the beach. It had little thatched roofs over each table—Kirk naturally knew that these were called *palapas*—and those big Mexican wicker chairs that are so wonderfully comfortable. With a candle on the table and the sun setting over the Pacific, whose waves almost splashed up to our table, it was really a lovely place.

The girls, too, looked lovely. For Nicole this required very little effort—she would have been gorgeous in paint-splattered track pants—but tonight she had on a sheer dress that seemed to swirl around her body quite effortlessly, both hiding and revealing the curves beneath. For Lacey, a little more work was required. She seemed fully recovered from her drinking the night before, and for tonight had done something with her makeup that made her eyes seem very large and her lips very full. I'm not sure how women perform such miracles with the various tubes, brushes, and lotions that seem to take up so much room in the bathroom, but they can work wonders. Lacey was actually attractive. In her tight tube-top and wrap-around skirt, she was also quite sexy.

And I'll admit it: the suggestion that Lacey might be "easy" or at least easy enough for me had subtly changed how I looked at her. Hanging out with her might be more than just a favour for my roommate, it might actually lead to something.

Dinner was quite pleasant sitting at our table as the surf bubbled towards us. Without the blaring mariachi band, the four of us could talk easily across the table. Nicole really was a very nice girl, I finally decided, who put on the ice queen attitude just to keep a world of horny men at bay. Given her looks, what other option did she have? She was bright, serious about her studies, and quite genuinely interested in Kirk's religious ideas. At times she even reminded me of Maggie. There was something about her shy smile and her quick wit, a bit caustic but a bit sweet, that had me remembering so many nights with Maggie back at home. I knew that Maggie would have loved it here at this restaurant on the edge of the Pacific.

But as Kirk so succinctly put it, Lacey was here and Maggie wasn't. There's fantasy and then there's opportunity. After taking care of the bill, Kirk and Nicole declared that they were going off for a last walk down the beach. That left me looking into Lacey's eyes.

"You know, Lacey, I am just beginning to appreciate how wonderful you really are."

"So you've forgiven me for last night?" she asked.

"Forgiven and forgotten," I told her. "And tonight I've really gotten to appreciate you. You're so much more interesting than I had ever dreamed."

"Really?" she giggled.

"Really," I replied, though it was a bit of an exaggeration. "I just wish we could spend more time together here. It's such a shame that you're flying home tomorrow."

"Me, too," she replied. "We could email."

"We will," I said with a wistful sigh. "But now this is our last night together, here in this beautiful place." And then I had a burst of inspiration.

The sea is calm to-night.
The tide is full, the moon lies fair
Upon the straits; on the French coast the light
Gleams and is gone; the cliffs of England stand,
Glimmering and vast, out in the tranquil bay.

Lacey's eyes lit up. "Oh, Alan, did you write that?"

"Well, actually," I began and got ready to give Matthew Arnold his due, but then something else clicked into my brain, "actually I did."

"So you write poetry?" she said.

"Not much," I told her. "I just try to capture certain moments."

"Like this one, tonight?"

Lacey's face was so bright and her gaze so focused on me that I couldn't back away. Somehow I was making an impression, a big impression, so I went ahead:

Ah, love, let us be true
To one another! For this world, which seems
To lie before us like a land of dreams,
So various, so beautiful, so new,
Tomorrow is lost in the northern snows.

Tomorrow I would apologize to the ghost of Matthew Arnold. But for now I just looked into Lacey's eyes, then took her into my arms and kissed her.

"Alan, let's go back to your room," she said, breaking away. "Let's not waste this last night."

"Oh, yes," I replied.

In seconds we were out of the restaurant and flagging down a cab. Clearly we both had sex in mind. I suspected that Lacey already had some experience in matters sexual, but I wasn't going to ask, and I certainly wasn't going to tell her that we were rushing off for my first real sex, ever. A man has to have some pride.

"Much better taxi ride than last night," I said, climbing in beside her.

"Oh shut up," she replied, giggling, then pressing her lips against mine.

So there was not a lot of witty repartee before we got back to the El Paradiso. By then, it was almost midnight and the hotel lobby was largely empty. Lacey and I could make our way to the elevator and upstairs with only a few eyes staring at us. I felt a bit embarrassed, but it was Spring Break, after all, so what could people expect?

We reached my shared hotel room on the fourth floor, staggering down the hall with our arms around each other's waists. I admit, I was both nervous and excited. All of the attempts at getting laid over the last two years, all of the grand plans and schemes that ultimately led to frustration, and now it was simply coming to me. There's that principle of irony, again.

I tried to think about how we'd do it. Go inside, close door, grope, remove clothes, find condom. No—find condom first, then have it ready so it doesn't break the mood. Fortunately I had no socks to worry about this time, no angry husbands or small children to break in on the action. It was just me, Al Macklin, and a girl so hot she could hardly keep her hands off me. This was it—the moment of truth.

Except that there was a shirt hanging on the room door.

"Oh, no," I said.

"What's the matter?"

"Somebody's inside," I explained. "I mean, one of the guys and a girl are in there, you know, kind of . . ."

"Like, doing it," Lacey concluded

"Right," I replied, blushing for no good reason.

Tap-tap-tippity-tap, I tapped. Did I remember the right pattern? I tried a quick variation. *Tap-tippity-tap- tap.* There, that should get the message across. There was even a grunt from inside to indicate that the message had been received.

"I have a hunch they'll be out of there in maybe ten or twenty minutes. Now what could we do to pass the time?"

Lacey smiled at me. "Like, make out?"

"Excellent suggestion," I replied.

I looked up and down the hall for some place that would give us a little privacy, but saw nothing obvious. So I took Lacey over to the wall just to the right of the door to our room, where we were shielded from public view by a fire extinguisher. All right, I guess we were not *much* shielded from public view, but it seemed a little cozier than making out right in the middle of the hall.

We were in mid-makeout when I heard a noise at the elevator. I decided that our foreplay should not be disturbed by minor annoyances like people trying to get to their rooms, so I continued. By now my hands were so busily involved with Lacey that, had she screamed, I would have been up on assault charges. But there was no scream, only mild moans of pleasure. Unfortunately, her sounds were soon joined by another.

"Ah-hem," was the sound. In truth, it was more of a cough or a throat-clearing, but the effect was the same.

I stopped kissing Lacey and looked to the left in the direction of the elevator doors.

"Alan, my man."

It was Scrooge. Naturally there was a girl with him. From the girl's outfit, it would seem that she had just been a contestant in a wet T-shirt contest.

"Uh, hello," I said.

"Passing the time?" he asked.

"I did the knock," I told him. "We're next in line."

"So who's inside?" Scrooge asked.

"Well, it has to be . . ." I began.

At that moment, the door to our room flew open and the couple inside appeared in the doorway. It was Kirk!

With Nicole!

My jaw dropped. I realize that's a cliché, but that is exactly what happened. In fact, Scrooge's jaw dropped. If the girls had realized how astonishing this was, I bet their jaws, too, would have dropped.

Instead, Lacey stared at Nicole.

"And what were you doing, Nikki?"

"I . . . uh . . ." Nicole stuttered. Under stress, all her self-confidence just disappeared.

"Sorry," Kirk said, his face reddening. "We were just talking."

"Talking?" Scrooge asked.

"Talking," Kirk repeated.

With anyone else, we would have all broken into laughter. With any other guy, there would have been lewd jokes and lots of rude suggestions followed by a reminder that their time was up. But with Kirk, we were all left repeating ourselves.

"Talking," I said.

"Talking," Kirk repeated.

"Talking?" Lacey asked.

"Talking," Scrooge added.

It was Nicole who broke the stunned repetition.

"Yes, we were talking," she said vehemently. "It's something that intelligent people do." Nicole stared at us, with the obvious suggestion that the rest of us—more interested in sex than conversation—were lacking in intelligence.

Had I been somewhat quicker in my mind, I might have noted that sex and intelligence were not mutually exclusive, that one can be horny and bright—indeed, horny and a genius—without any contradiction. But I was a bit dulled by alcohol, so I said nothing as Nicole took over.

"Alan, get your hands off Lacey. She's leaving with me."

"She is?" I asked, dumbly.

"I am?" Lacey echoed.

"She is and you are," Nicole ordered. With that, she grabbed Lacey by the arm and led her towards the elevator. In a few seconds, the elevator chimed, the door opened, and the two girls disappeared.

Scrooge shook his head. "Smoked ya," he said succinctly.

"Yeah," I sighed.

Then he took the hand of his girl and smiled at Kirk and me. "Now, gentlemen, if we could take our turn?"

22

New Vows

I BELIEVE KIRK AND NICOLE *were* talking, and mostly *just* talking. The other guys may have had different opinions, based on excessive reading of men's magazines like *Maxim*, but I probably know my roommate better than anyone, or anyone except Nicole. If Kirk says they were talking, and he tells me they just wanted a quiet place for some serious talking, then I believe him.

"Yeah, like he was really talking," Matt said with scorn the next day. Kirk had gone jogging down the beach so missed this conversation. "You don't go into a room with a girl like that and just talk. Let me tell you what I would do."

"Spare us," Scrooge said, cutting him off. "From my experience, talking can sometimes be better than sex."

We stared at him, open-mouthed.

"Sometimes," Scrooge repeated with a certainty that made the rest of us fall silent.

It was our fourth day or maybe the fifth day of a seven-day holiday. I confess, I had lost count. The sun had already done its damage to most of us; the tequila was taking its toll on our collective brains; Nicole and Lacey had flown home; and I had given up on getting laid.

One by one, almost all the other guys in our crew found a girl—during their stay. Make that three or four in Scrooge's case. Matt hooked up with a very cute, very petite girl from Chicago. Biff connected with a girl who looked like a female bodybuilder. Aiden found a curly-haired history major from Utah, of all places. And Goofball found a group of stoners to hang out with, spending a lot of time with a much tattooed and much pierced girl whose eyes seemed permanently glazed over—and not from romance.

Even Fuji—and that was the most grating thing—found a girl. By our fourth day, he was joined at the hip to a tiny Asian girl who seemed to play video games as well as Fuji. Even Scrooge had to shake his head. "The man must be dynamite with a joystick."

In the face of their success I proclaimed that virginity really was a good thing.

"I could have told you that," Kirk said. We had found a bar that served one-dollar Scotches and I was busy tossing them back. My only satisfaction was that Kirk had to pay two dollars for each of his Cokes.

"It gives me an innocence," I said, "a freshness."

"No risk of pregnancy or disease," Kirk added.

"No pretense of commitment."

"Absolutely right," Kirk agreed.

"But still," I moaned, "I think I'm the last nineteen-year-old virgin on the planet."

"Correction," Kirk said. "There are two of us."

We decided that there was some larger force at work preserving my virginity. Kirk would say that God had other intentions for his servant Alan, that my calling was higher than fleshly desire. But that would be Kirk talking. I simply finished up the holiday feeling frustrated, philosophy or no.

On the plane flight home, Kirk was sitting beside me, looking more tanned and handsome than ever. Fuji was behind us again, playing video games.

"You know, Al, I've got to thank you for this experience."

"You do?"

"Absolutely," Kirk said. "I got a chance to get over Kathy and I got to meet a girl who's even more wonderful. I was able to learn about the evils of tequila and rum. And I got an early tan."

"Well, bully for you," I snapped.

"Don't be so down," he went on. "There is more to life than sex, Al. Just because you didn't get a girl doesn't mean the holiday was a failure. It was what it was. You had the experience the good Lord wanted you to have."

I hate it when Kirk goes religious-philosophical on me, so I decided to cut him short.

"I'm going to make a vow, Father Kirk," I said.

"Wrong church," he told me, "but I'll be happy to listen."

"I vow to give up on women until the summer," I said. My fingers were not crossed. I was, despite my hangover, deadly earnest.

"That's just a couple of months," Kirk reminded me.

"True, but this is a real vow. I will not date, chat up, or pursue any female for the remainder of this school year. In fact, I will do my best not to *think* about any female for the next few months."

"This is serious, Al. Maybe we should write it down."

So on the back of a TransitAir napkin, I scribbled my vow.

> *I will not pursue, chat up, or date any female for the remainder of this school year.*
>
> *—Alan Macklin*

I signed my name with a flourish.

"So what are you going to do instead?" Kirk asked.

"Maybe I'll meditate."

Kirk gave me a look just as the stewardess came by to offer us drinks. She gave Kirk a wonderful, winning smile. She gave me an orange juice.

"Still, meditation wouldn't be bad," Kirk said. "I think you could stand a little more looking inside instead of ogling outside."

"Meaning?"

"Maybe the romance you want isn't out there," Kirk said. "Maybe what you're seeking isn't some airhead like Lacey, or some older woman who's out of your league. Maybe you really want something more serious, a girl you really care about."

"Spare me," I sighed. "My goal is simple. I want to get laid."

"Is it really that simple?"

"Of course it's simple," I mumbled. "I'm a simple guy . . . with a simple goal . . . it's really very simple . . ." and then I nodded off to sleep.

I had a weird dream while I was sleeping. It involved a Mexican beach, and some little girl crying, and Lacey, who then turned into an awful old woman, and a taxicab driver demanding a hundred dollars. And then his face turned into Matthew Arnold's face looking angry that I'd stolen his poem and pretended it was mine. It was his face that made me wake up with a start. And that was when I had my moment of inspiration.

"I've got it," I said. If I'd been a Greek philosopher, I would have shouted *Eureka*!

"Got what?" Kirk asked.

"I've got an idea." I replied. "I'm going to write poetry."

"Not a bad idea, Al." Kirk said cheerfully. "You begin writing poetry and you might start thinking with your brain instead of your, uh, you know."

"Yeah, I might," I told him. "It might be a brand new experience."

"It could be deep," he said.

"Or shallow," I replied. "But it'll be more than what I've got right now."

I did not begin my new career as a poet immediately, however. Plane flights do not inspire poetry. Nor did my return to school. There were other matters to deal with—midterms, assignments, readings, all the dull stuff of university life. It was difficult to find quiet, contemplative moments to begin my poetic work. I mean, you just don't knock off a poem while running from Taylor Hall to the quad; you have to meditate and wait for inspiration. Keats and Shelley, for instance, went off to Italy for inspiration. Perhaps if I had gone to Italy rather than Puerto Vallarta I, too, would be moved to pen a few great lines.

Instead, I sent email. Email was so much easier.

From: amacklin@BU.edu
To: maggiemac@sl.edu
Back from PV, virginity intact. Despite my best efforts using wit, charm, and tequila, the Spring Break girls managed to resist me. Did manage to get a decent sunburn and a few fine hangovers, but surely there is more to life than that.

Roommate Kirk, incidentally, managed to rebound from the departure of one flawless female by lucking into a second flawless female. Apparently she goes to your school. Does the name Nicole something-or-other ring a bell? She's your basic blonde type, perfect skin, perfect cheekbones, perfect everything. Kind of boring unless perfect is your thing.

Scrooge sends his love. Of course he sends every girl his love. What makes that guy so sexy and me so not?

From: maggiemac@sl.edu
To: amacklin@BU.edu
Al, you are sexy, but not in a conventional way. You just need somebody to discover how sexy you really are. Scrooge simply has a confidence that's appealing. Nothing to be jealous of.

The shocker in your email was the reference to Nicole Johanssen, known around here as the Ice Queen. She fits the description, and impresses all the rest of us as hopelessly vain and stuck-up. Kirk must really be something to have melted the ice wall, kind of like Prince Calaf managing to seduce Turandot.

Send me salacious details.

From: amacklin@BU.edu
To: maggiemac@sl.edu
Turandot who? I must cluelessly ask. As for salacious details, all I can report is that Nicole and Kirk emerged

from our shared hotel room in a somewhat dishevelled state. Good word, eh? Kirk maintains that they were just talking, and I believe him, but others suspect that there were sheet-rumpling activities going on. Anyhow, it's turned into a full-blown romance with letters flying across the continent (Kirk doesn't do email, remember), etc., etc. She even sent him flowers one day. Made our room smell quite lovely for almost a week.

From: maggiemac@sl.edu
To: amacklin@BU.edu
Turandot from the opera by Puccini, you delightful dolt. The flower gesture is really quite touching. Sounds like your roommate won her heart, to the extent that Nicole has a heart. Incidentally, if you ever get in the mood to send flowers this way, I'd be happy to receive same. Saw Nicole the other day and mentioned Kirk's name in passing. Her flawless white skin turned bright pink in response, a sure sign of romance.

Your bit of gossip has done wonders for my social standing around here. Apparently anyone who knows anything about Nicole Johanssen goes ahead two big squares on the social game board. Keep any gossip coming my way. If this continues, I may even end up popular.

Incidentally, I've decided to become a philosophy major, destined for a career of worthy unemployment. This will give me time to contemplate the significant issues of life, society, and the moral universe. Should work well with my new hermetic existence. Too bad you're not an aspiring Jean-Paul Sartre, I could be your Simone de Beauvoir.

From: amacklin@BU.edu
To: maggiemac@sl.edu
Have decided to become a poet and thereby join you in contemplating the significant issues of life, society, and the moral universe. Unfortunately, I had to look up "hermetic" so I fear that my vocabulary may not measure up to the demands of the poetic muses. Also having a heck of a time writing my first poem, but I'm sure it's developing subconsciously. The muses can't be rushed, I'm told. They show up on their own timetable, so I'm trying not to be impatient.

23

The Muses

THE GREEKS SAID that there were nine muses, three of whom gave inspiration to poets. Surely, I thought, one of the three would begin to speak through me. I kept priming the pump, reading Keats and Shelley, Tennyson and Wordsworth, even T. S. Eliot and Ezra Pound and Lawrence Ferlinghetti. I picked up little magazines at the library that were full of difficult, obscure poems by contemporary poets. Surely, I told myself, with all this pump-priming, the waters of poesy would soon pour forth.

But no poetry gushed from my soul, or my computer, until a lovely April day on campus. I was sitting outside Sloppy Joe's, trying to keep a pizza slice from slipping onto my shirt, when the muse finally sang. There was, I must admit, a little immediate inspiration. Walking down the quad was a particularly gorgeous girl whose streaked hair glowed golden in the sunlight. I watched her pass, trying not to be too obvious in my ogling, and then admired her as she walked off to class. It was that moment when the muse gave me my first line of poetry:

Like a fresh peach, her perfect skin hints at the
luscious girl beneath.

That was it. The line seemed more William Carlos Williams than Keats or Shelley, but I wasn't going to complain.

"Al, you're smiling," Kirk said when I came into our room. "You find some girl to help you break your vow?"

I shook my head. "You of little faith," I said. "My vow is intact. I'm smiling because the muses have begun to sing."

"The muses?"

"The poetic muses," I explained. "Remember I said that I was going to be a poet? Well, I've been having a little trouble with, like, actually writing something. So today, for the first time, I got inspired. You ready for the line?"

Kirk nodded and I delivered my first line of verse.

"Is that it?" Kirk asked.

"Yeah, so far."

"So there's going to be more?"

I snorted. "Of course there's going to be more. Who ever heard of a one-line poem? I just have to flesh out the poem a little."

"Uh, right," Kirk said, trying to be noncommittal. "I picked up a package for you at the mailroom. I think it's from my sister."

There, on my bed, was a package wrapped in plain brown paper. Kirk got roses from his girlfriend; I got a brown-paper package. This was just the nature of life, I kept telling myself, and I'd better get used to it.

I opened the package and found that it contained a letter, a book, and a ring—the TLW ring.

"This is not good news, Kirk," I told him. The ring seemed clear enough, but if I was unclear on the message, the book brought it home. It was a self-help book entitled *Sixty Ways to Leave Your Lover.*

Kirk was curious and came over beside me. "I don't like the look of this," he said.

I unfolded the letter and read it aloud.

Dear Alan,
I'm tried of waiting. You could have come to see me over Spring Break, but instead you head off to Mexico with my brother. Why didn't you invite me, you jerk?

I cried, Al. Honestly, I cried. I've been waiting for you. You were going to be the one, the very first one.

But you waited too long. There's a new guy in my life, and he didn't make me wait until the summer. You had your chance, Al, but you weren't quick enough.

Here's your ring back. Maybe you can use it with the next girl. This one just got tired of waiting.
Patti

The dot over the *i* in Patti's name came complete with a little smiley face sticking out its tongue at me.

"Al, you've just been dumped," Kirk said.

"Scorned," I said, using the poetic turn.

"Are you heartbroken?"

"Working on it."

"Crestfallen?"

"Definitely."

"And now my father has a problem," Kirk concluded. "I'd better give him a call about Pug."

In truth, I felt very little when I read Patti's letter, the most significant emotion being relief. I guess our pseudo-romance had managed to preserve her virginity for another three months or so, but the girl was destined for real sex sooner or later and I had just made it a little bit later.

But I liked the idea of being a scorned lover. If love is the source of most poetry, then scorned love must be the second most promising inspiration. I took out my pen and began to write.

Like a fresh peach, her perfect skin hints at the
luscious girl beneath,
Like an azure sky, her clear eyes speak of deep
pools within,
Like a crimson sun, her lips whisper of hopes and
dreams to come.

But no more! She scorns me now with those perfect lips,
Her eyes are fixed on another, her skin caressed by
his hand,
Not mine, and I am left longing for one more touch
of those sweet lips.

Maybe not a great poem, but not bad for my very first effort, if I do say so myself. I decided to celebrate the event by emailing Maggie.

From: amacklin@BU.edu
To: maggiemac@sl.edu
Have completed poem number one! Also been dumped by Kirk's sister, and maybe that was the inspiration. If there's one thing I know about, it's being dumped by women. Isn't that the first rule of writing—write what you know about? I may not know about Mount Parnassus or the art of Tuscany or the moors of England, but I do know what it's like to be scorned.

I finished my email and then went on to write two more poems. I was on a roll! Admittedly, poems two and three were a bit rough—more collections of random thoughts than polished poems—but, heck, who was I to put down random thoughts? They were certainly better than no thoughts.

From: maggiemac@sl.edu
To: amacklin@BU.edu
So when do I get to see this poem? Surely you are not going to hide your light under the proverbial bushel. Besides, you might have a great future as a poet for the rejected and forlorn. Simple success is so boring, but striving and failing is what gives meaning to our lives.

Also decided to take an intensive French course when school ends. Two weeks in Chicoutimi should make me sufficiently bilingual to at least order a hamburger, if not read Sartre in the original. Ergo: won't see you until June. Tell me that you'll miss me. Better yet, write me a poem that says you'll miss me.

On a more mundane note, I have decided to dye my hair black. I've decided that redheads do not command the respect and attention given to those with darker hair colours. Rather than complain about discrimination and prejudice, I'm going to try life as a brunette. Giving up the contacts, too. Serious people wear glasses and I'm redefining myself as a serious person. You may not recognize me when next we meet, my friend.

I tried to imagine Maggie with dark hair, and failed. But when I thought about her, a whole set of words started floating up in my mind—or maybe they were feelings trying to find words. So I started another poem, this one about Maggie, and it turned out to be a sonnet. Okay, it wasn't a rhyming sonnet, but it had fourteen lines and was vaguely romantic. Then I got another idea, and quickly scribbled down the rough version of a second sonnet.

Maybe I am a poet, I said to myself after all these poems were in my computer. I mean, how many poems does a guy have to write to qualify?

24

Farewell and Welcome

In May, the school year ended, and it was time to pack up our gear for the flights home. I finished up my first year at BU as an A-minus student, which was more than decent, given my relatively poor mark in Philosophy 101. Officially, I had learned something about the oppression of women throughout history, the development of poetry in the eighteenth and nineteenth centuries, the role of enquiry in the dialogues of Plato, and the importance of feminist avatars in films of the 1940s. Unofficially, I learned about tequila, single-malt Scotch, cigars, older women, younger women, drinking, and hangovers.

But what did I really learn? I learned that I would never be a Kirk. I learned that there really are people who are serious about themselves, and what they want, and what they believe in. My roommate never failed to impress me, right up to that final week when he broke the terrible news.

"You're what? I demanded.

"I'm transferring," he said. "There's a Christian college back in Calgary that's got a perfect program for me."

"You're going where?" I shrieked.

"Honestly, it was a tough decision. I've been thinking about all this, what I'm learning here, and what I want for myself. And it wasn't easy, Al, but I think I've explored the pagan side enough," he told me.

"Your haven't explored the half of it," I shot back. "I mean, there's falling down drunk and kinky sex and weird drugs and . . . I mean there's lots more to pagan than you've seen so far. You haven't even scratched the surface."

"I've seen enough, Al," he said. "I have to admit, there's an attraction to it. That's what I felt down in Puerto Vallarta, the pull of temptation. It's powerful stuff. Satan has always been powerful. If I stay here, I may not be strong enough to resist."

"Kirk, you've already resisted plenty."

"But I'm weakening," he said. "And I want to concentrate more on my Bible studies. The context here is all wrong. There's too much history and anthropology and not enough faith."

"Faith," I repeated.

"Yeah, faith. It's important to me."

"I know." I was losing this argument. In truth, I had probably lost the argument a couple months before.

"Still, I'm going to miss you, Al. You've been a great friend and opened my eyes to so many things. I don't ever want us to lose touch. Whatever happens, we've got to stay in touch."

"You don't do email," I said.

"So buy some stamps," Kirk replied.

"But next year I'll have to get a new roommate, and God knows who I'll end up with," I whined.

Kirk gave me that patronizing church minister look. "God does know, Al, and it'll be fine."

So there I was, dumped by my own roommate, and feeling pretty miserable about it. When I flew back home, I was able to add three more poems to my "scorned" collection. I had made the best friend of my life, and lost him in just a year. Is that fair? I ask in a very unpoetic fashion. About as fair as going to Puerto Vallarta for Spring Break and coming back with my virginity intact.

Even the plane flight home was bad. I had a middle seat. Why do they even assign middle seats? The middle seats in planes should be reserved for use by very small people in case of emergency; they should never be used for gangly university students. But there I was, trapped between an older lady who had decided that both armrests belonged to her, and a large businessman in the aisle seat who was clicking away at his computer, elbows spread sideways.

Maybe travelling in my parents' car wasn't all that bad.

When we touched down, the plane taxied for twenty minutes before coming to the gate, then the various sardines packed in the aluminum can wriggled in their seats, stood up, and prepared to exit. The actual exit, however, was delayed because the pilot hadn't pulled the plane forward enough, so we had to go through the landing procedure again before we were free to walk up the vile-smelling ramp to the airport itself.

Next time, I told myself, I'll take the train. Except there aren't trains anymore.

But I got a surprise when I got to the baggage area—it wasn't just my parents waiting for me, there was a welcoming committee: Scrooge, Jeremy, Hannah the Honker, and Allison the Gorgeous.

Scrooge gave me one of his enormous smiles. "We heard you were coming, my man, so Hannah baked you a cake."

"A small cake," Hannah said, handing me a cupcake. "Actually, I bought it at the coffee shop, but you know the expression: it's the thought that counts. Maggie sends her love, but she's studying French, or something, for another couple of weeks."

I looked at them open-mouthed. It was the entire membership of Maggie's Friday film society except Maggie herself. Scrooge was the same as ever—cool and assured—but the others had changed. Jeremy, the guy whose advice about girls had proved so unreliable, looked almost respectable. He'd put on twenty pounds, but his hair seemed less greasy and there was no longer the hint of spittle on his lips. Hannah, known as "the Honker" for her large nose, had become quite attractive—nose and all. Maybe it was something about makeup and hairstyle, but Hannah was now worth a second look. Maybe a third look. And Allison, always the most beautiful girl in our high school, seemed a little tired. There were dark circles under her eyes, which kind of spoiled her usual Angelina Jolie perfection, and her hair was cut in a strange way. She remained gorgeous, despite all this, but a bit more human than she'd been even a year ago.

"So, welcome home," Allison said, kissing my cheek.

"Yeah, welcome home, dude," Scrooge said. For a second I was afraid he might kiss my other cheek, but that would have been over the top.

"Welcome home, Alan," chimed in my mother, looking unusually cheerful. From her expression, you might even have thought she missed me.

My father didn't add to the welcomes. He was off chasing my first piece of luggage, which was circling on the baggage conveyor.

"I don't know what to say," I told them, probably blushing a little.

"You're a poet, my man," Scrooge replied. "You're supposed to know what to say."

Hannah asked the obvious: "So how many poems have you written, Al?"

"Thirty, give or take," I replied.

"Thirty?" Allison asked. "Thirty poems?" Her blue eyes looked at me with something that I took to be admiration.

"Some are fragments. Some aren't even close to finished," I admitted.

"Hey, man, that's not bad," Scrooge said with a little real admiration. "I mean, you've made almost as many poems this year as . . . uh . . ."

"As you've made girls."

He smiled. "Yeah, right."

My dad came up with my two suitcases at this point. I told him there was one more thing, a computer box that actually had most of my stuff. It was amazing how much I'd collected in just nine months away. If Kirk had been staying on, we would have gotten an apartment and kept the stuff out west, but as it was I'd be heading back to the dorms for my second year and there was no summer storage.

I can't say that I was looking forward to a summer back in my parents' house. On the bright side, my father had managed to score a job for me with the city public works department. This was a cut up from my previous work at Dairy Queen. On the dark side, my job involved emptying trash bins from the local parks. I suppose there was some justice in this, since my three years of work at Dairy Queen had been entirely devoted to making trash for the bins I would now be emptying.

Still, it was a unionized job so the pay was good—almost seventeen dollars an hour, double my old pay at Dairy Queen. The money would give me a rich life at school and perhaps another Mexican vacation next spring.

In a week, I had settled back into the life I'd lived in high school, except for the school itself. I began IM-ing again, since all my friends—except Maggie—were so close, and even talking by cell phone now that I could afford a decent plan. I began hanging out with the old crew. We went to movies and hit the bars after work, and held our Friday night popcorn and black-and-white film festival at Allison's house with her new, big plasma-screen television.

"How's the trashman today?" Scrooge asked as we were settling in one Friday. Trashman was my new nickname. This Friday's film was Jean Renoir's *La grande illusion*. It was the kind of movie that Maggie would have picked, though the actual choice was made by Hannah.

"The Trashman is beat," I told them.

"You know," Scrooge told me, "Trashman wouldn't be a bad name for a rapper. It's kind of like being a poet, Al. I can see you doing it: Trashman, right up there with Snoop Dogg and Jay Z."

"If I could rap," I said, getting in the mood, "I'd be the candy wrapper rapper."

"Not bad, my man," Scrooge replied. "How about I give you the backup." He began doing that generic rap rhythm, kind of bump-ba-ba-bump-ba-ba-bump, except it came with various kinds of pops and whistles.

So I began to join in:

Jujubes, Mr. Big, candy bars galore,
M&Ms and Mars bars, right from the store.
My back's near broke from picking up that stuff,
But my boss just says . . . that's real tough.

There was an amazed round of applause from the others.

"You ever think about doing some public poetry, you know, some performance poetry?" Allison asked.

I winced. "Not ready for prime time," I sighed.

"First, Al's got to get laid," Scrooge threw in.

"Right," I agreed. "Got to keep my priorities straight."

"Well, I was just wondering," she said. "I pulled this from the bulletin board up at the college. Looks like they're having a poetry slam at the student union pub next week."

We all looked at the flyer.

SEAMUS CALHOUN'S POETRY SLAM

Poets, versifiers, rappers, and ministory-tellers—come to Calhoun's first poetry slam of the summer. The rules are simple; the rewards are preposterous!

1. Poets must perform poems of their own creation—no plagiarism, please. Poems may be of any style, including formal verse, free verse, monologues, sonnets, parables, ballads, stream-of-consciousness rambles, rants and raps, hip-hop meditations, romantic wordgasms, dirty limericks, sparse and lean haiku, fables, twisted tales, iambic pentameter sonnets, napkin-scribbled words of wisdom, improvised words of anger, beat-box verse, abstract-experimental lyricism, and drunken drivel—to mention just a few.
2. No props, costumes, musical accompaniment, or animal acts are allowed on stage. Poets are limited to their own devices and talents. Three-minute time limit. Audience response is invited . . . and not part of the time limit.
3. A group of three judges selected from the audience scores each poem on a scale of 0.0 to 10.0, considering both content and performance.
4. High scores advance to second and third rounds.
5. The grand prize . . . a keg of ale (or a reasonable equivalent).

"You should do it, Al," Jeremy told me. "Not only will your poetry be a slam-dunk success, but you'll sweep the women off their feet. Once their feet are off the ground, the rest is easy."

"Jeremy, do you mind?" Hannah snapped.

"Sorry," Jeremy said, looking down at his feet.

"But you could do it, Al," Allison said, ignoring Jeremy and picking up the thread. "All you need is three or four poems, good ones, and you're set. We'd all come out to cheer you on."

"Thanks, but—"

"Don't see what the buts are about, Al," said Jeremy. "You *said* you had thirty poems."

"Not all complete."

"But thirty poems," Jeremy went on. "You only need three or four, and just one good one. You do have *one* good poem, don't you?"

All the eyes turned to me. This was becoming truly embarrassing. I thought I had a dozen pretty good poems, but I'd never read them out loud to anyone. I hadn't even shared them with Maggie.

"These things are about performance," I told them. I was squirming on the couch like a worm on the sidewalk. "I'm not a performer. I just write."

Scrooge jumped in. "Al, I have seen you do some pretty smooth talking, my friend. Anybody who can snow women the way you do can certainly belt a poem out to a crowd. It's the same thing, my man."

"You were quite good as the Wall in *Midsummer Night's Dream*," Allison added brightly.

I remembered the role. Scrooge was Pyramus; Allison was Thisby; and I was the wall that separated the lovers. I even remembered my lines: *"That I, one Snout by name, present a wall; And such a wall, as I would have you think, That had in it a crannied hole or chink."* That was my entire role. Maybe I was good, but it wasn't much of a challenge.

"You were a good tree in that grade-seven play," Jeremy added.

"I've only ever played a tree or a wall in my entire acting career," I whined.

"Start with the easy parts and get to the character roles later," Scrooge threw in, and there was more laughter.

But Allison wouldn't let the matter drop. "Alan, I really think you should do it. Win or lose, we'll all be there to support you. And it'll be fun."

I looked up at her. "Fun?"

"Yeah, fun," she said. "I think all of us have forgotten how to have fun this year. We've become too serious."

"Hear, hear," said Jeremy, imitating his father.

"Sadly true," added Scrooge. "Even for me."

Allison spoke in her serious, pay-attention-to-me voice. "I'll sign you up for the poetry slam," she said, "and if you need help rehearsing, just let me know. I actually promised Maggie I'd give you a little help before the big night. She says you'll need it."

"So Maggie wants me to do it, too?"

"She insists," Allison declared.

I sighed, twisted, hemmed and hawed, but the matter was decided. I give in too easily to women—that's my problem.

"Now can we start this artsy film?" Jeremy demanded. "I want to get beyond the popcorn and into some serious food."

So we watched *La grande illusion*, and I tried to pay attention. I tried to use the analytical skills I'd learned in Film 101 to make sense of Jean Renoir's classic. But my mind was only half on the movie, the other half was on my poetry and the poetry slam. To put it simply, I was terrified.

25

Slammed

The night of the poetry slam, I spent a little time deciding on my clothes. Black, I thought, would be good. Serious. Dark. Full of meaning. I had a black buttoned shirt and a black T-shirt and I was trying to choose between them when my father stuck his head in the bedroom doorway.

"Al, I know you're going out tonight—" he began.

"Yeah," I said, choosing the T-shirt. A more muscular look, I thought. More like James Dean. Maybe I should buy a pack of cigarettes and stick them under one sleeve. Who cares if I don't know how to smoke. It might improve the look.

"Your mom and I wanted to have a little talk with you, before you go."

I looked up. My father has always been awkward talking to me, and this was no exception. He stood there nervously, shifting his weight from one foot to another.

"It has to be tonight?" I asked. "I've got a few things on my mind."

"So do we," he said. "It shouldn't take long."

I finished getting dressed, then debated the issue of cologne but decided that a real poet wouldn't use any. A real poet would hardly even shower, I figured, certainly not if he wanted to look like James Dean.

So I stumbled down the stairs at seven-thirty, wondering what my parents were so desperate to discuss. We hardly ever discussed anything in my family, and never if there were some way to delay it. I had offered my father the option of a breakfast discussion, but got a simple no. So now I was curious. More words of wisdom? My father hadn't given me any words about anything since dropping me off at school in the fall. Perhaps he'd been saving up.

My mom and dad were both in the living room when I got there. They looked uncomfortable.

"What's up?" I asked.

"Al, you better sit down," my dad began.

"Is this, like, serious?" I had twenty immediate images running through my brain: my parents are getting divorced, my mom has breast cancer, my dad has prostate cancer, the house is being sold, a tornado is on the way . . . Sometimes my imagination gets the better of me.

"Well, I think it's good news, really. Just a surprise," my mother said.

"A surprise? A good surprise?"

"Well, mostly good," my dad came in. "You see, we went to the doctor a few months ago and found out, well, we're not sure how it happened, really, and wanted to make sure everything was alright . . ." his voice dropped off.

It was my mother who blurted out the news. "I'm pregnant," she said. Then she smiled and her cheeks turned pink.

"Pregnant!" I shrieked.

"Pregnant," she repeated.

"Pregnant, like how?" I asked.

"Oh, Alan, surely you know how. The teachers cover that in school, don't they," my mom said.

"But after all dad's talk about being careful and protection and all that . . ." I was at a loss for words.

"Accidents happen," my father said with a shrug. "Al, in November you're going to have a little brother or sister."

"A little brother or sister," I said, mostly to myself. "I'll be a big brother. A *really* big brother. I mean, there's going to be twenty years between us."

"A bit of a gap," my dad admitted.

"Yeah, you could say that," I replied.

I suppose we could have kept on talking for a while, and certainly there were plenty of questions swirling through my brain, but Scrooge's car horn was beeping from the driveway.

"We can talk more tomorrow," my mom said.

"Yeah, tomorrow," I replied. "Tonight I've got to . . ." for a moment, I couldn't even remember where I was going. Then it came back: the poetry slam. "Tonight I've got to go read some poetry."

My parents gave me a look of disbelief. It must have matched my earlier look of disbelief. But really, which of us was totally crazy? It certainly wasn't me.

Seamus Calhoun's—the campus pub—was only half-filled the night of the poetry slam. That was good. But almost everyone I knew had shown up—that was bad. I carried a clutch of poems in my hand. I was still not sure which ones I would read out, so I'd brought every poem I'd written, including the ridiculous Mars bar rap, just in case.

Scrooge drove me up to the pub, then brought me to the murky and beer-reeking interior. In the darkness, I could see that the Friday film society was already seated at its table, and nearby was another group of kids I went to high school with. If I messed up, there'd be plenty of witnesses.

"Stop shaking so much," Allison told me. "If you'd come over to rehearse, you'd have more confidence."

"Yeah, well . . ." I mumbled. I had been too scared to actually practise at Allison's house. She might have laughed. I would have died. It wasn't worth death by embarrassment to get a little advice.

"You'll be great, Al," Hannah came in. "Trust your inspiration. We're all on your side. All of us, plus one."

"Plus who?" I asked.

"Somebody who flew into town early, just for this," Hannah told me. "Look."

And there she was, showing her ID at the door.

"Maggie!" I cried.

Maggie looked spectacular. This was not the skinny Maggie I'd played soccer with a dozen years ago, not the kind-of-goofy-looking

Maggie I'd dated for my last year of high school, not the sad Maggie who'd been so forlorn at Christmas. This was a serious woman, a spectacular woman with dark hair, high cheekbones, gorgeous pale skin, and flashing blue eyes behind her very new, very stylish glasses.

"Maggie, you are such a hottie," Scrooge said with some appreciation. He and Maggie exchanged air-kisses, French style.

"Whoo-ee!" whistled Jeremy, eyeballing her short dress.

"No kisses for you Jeremy," Maggie replied. "But, Alan," she said, kissing my cheeks, "it's been too long."

Maggie sat down and the dress rode up a bit on her legs. *When did Maggie get such great legs*? I wondered.

I might just have stared at her, ogling, but Allison got us all down to business. "Okay, Alan, listen up. The poetry slam is going to start pretty soon, so you've got to get ready. Here's your number."

"My number?"

"Every poet gets a number, so you know exactly when you're going to read in the first round," Allison explained. "There are twelve poets, so you're on near the middle. Only five poets make the second round. And then there's the final round, for the grand prize."

"Free beer for a year!" Scrooge declared.

That was not actually true. The grand prize was more like twelve free pitchers of beer to be drunk over the summer. Still, such a prize was not to be dismissed. Given the recent news at home, I could use all the beer I could get.

"Let me pin the number on your shirt," Maggie said. As she got close, I got a whiff of her new perfume and a up-close view of her face. Her last semester away at Sarah Lawrence had done wonders for her, or maybe it was the couple of weeks in Chicoutimi, or maybe it was just life itself.

"Hey, Al, you look like you're going to be in a dance contest," Scrooge said.

"Kind of like Richard Gere, but without the tux," Jeremy added.

There was general laughter at my embarrassment, and I might otherwise have said something witty, but I just felt stunned. When too much stuff comes at me too fast, I panic. Like a deer on the highway, I just stare at the oncoming headlights. The way things were going, I might end up a venison steak at the end of the night.

I looked around the room and saw numbers being pasted on a dozen other poets. They ranged from pimply-faced students to serious-looking guys with greasy hair and glasses to old ladies who looked like my grandmother. I was still looking around the room when I saw one other face I knew, a frigid blast from my own dating past: Melissa Halvorsen.

Melissa was one of the first girls I'd ever gone out with in high school, and my general ineptness caused both of us some embarrassment. She hadn't spoken to me since then, so I was surprised to see her at the pub. I wondered if she was actually old enough to drink.

Amazingly, she walked right up to where I was sitting.

"I heard you were reading some poetry," she said. Her voice was flat and cold.

"Yeah, right," I replied.

"So I got my new boyfriend to bring me over," she went on, now smiling. "I just want to see you make a fool of yourself, Al. I want you to show the world what a loser you really are."

"Hey, hey," Scrooge said, jumping up.

Melissa quickly backed off. Still, this seemed another poor augury of things to come.

Augury. Got to use that word in a poem sometime.

"Alan, don't pay any attention to that gormless chicklet," Maggie announced. "I'm sorry I ever introduced you two."

Then Scrooge changed the subject. He raised his glass, cleared his throat and acted like the guy who proposes a toast at a wedding. "Ladies and gentlemen, lovers of poetry, friends . . ."

"Get on with it," Hannah sighed.

"I have a message, sent by ExpressPost, to give encouragement to our friend Alan. If I may read . . ."

The table grew relatively quiet. Scrooge got up and pulled a letter from his pocket with a gesture that resembled a flourish. Then he began.

"This is from Al's roommate at BU. I called to tell him about the poetry slam tonight and he sent this message: 'Alan, I know you've found your poetic voice. Tonight is the night to use it. Speak from your heart and the good Lord will be on your side. Your friend, Kirk Chamberlain.'"

There was a brief round of applause from my friends, and then the lights dimmed for the poetry slam itself.

An announcer got up to the microphone, blew into the mike several times, and then went through the rules of the evening. He was remarkable only because of a very painful stammer when he spoke, one of those stammers that keeps the audience on the edge of their seats wondering if the person will ever actually complete the word with which he is struggling. Thus the rules took far longer than would be allowed for any of the poets.

At last, the announcer reached into a goldfish bowl full of folded paper chits and selected three judges for the contest. Amazingly, one of the names picked was Scrooge.

"Alan," Scrooge whispered to me as he got up to take his new position, "this will be good for you."

I nodded grimly.

The judges took their chairs at a special table, and poet number one proceeded to the stage. This poet was an older man with a salt-and-pepper beard. He looked awkward perched up on a bar stool under a glaring spotlight.

"This poem is dedicated to my wife," he began, smiling out into the audience, "and it begins like this." There was a pause and he began to read a charming rhymed poem that was not about his wife, at all, but about a waterfall in Portugal. It was an okay poem, I thought, but had too much alliteration and at least five clichés that I could count. Nonetheless, he got a pleasant round of applause when he was finished, much of it coming from a middle-aged woman to our immediate left.

Poet number two looked too young to be permitted into the pub, but he must have gotten by the ID check somehow. He was a wide-faced boy with reddish hair and a dusting of freckles whose most interesting feature was an absence of eyebrows, which gave him a strange appearance onstage. His poem was a rant, addressed to his English teacher, which included more swear words than most of us would use in a month of serious cursing. When he finished, there was a smattering of applause before he sat down.

"No competition yet," Maggie whispered to me.

"Right," I said. But the question playing through my mind was, what poem was I going to read? Did I dare read the poem that I really wanted to read?

The third poet was a man dressed like a rapper though he was quite soft-spoken when he got to the microphone. He read a very traditional ode to his mother, and I thought the poem was really quite good. Poet number three contrasted with the fourth poet, a young man with greasy hair who delivered a sound poem entitled "Revving Intestines." I can't recall the words, even though there weren't many of them, but the sounds were quite spectacular, ranging from the *Rrrrrr* of a growling stomach, to various clicks and pops, to explosive hiccups and other bodily noises.

My mother would not have approved, but the crowd loved his poem. A whole table of people to our right got up and gave poet number four a standing ovation. I had nothing to compete with it.

Then it was time for poet number five—me. Shakily, I made my way up to the stage. I looked back at our tables, at the sea of smiling faces, and then caught a glimpse of Melissa Halvorsen, who was mentally shooting daggers at me. It was her scowl that helped me choose the poem.

"I, uh, is this mike on?" I began, awkwardly. "I'd like to read a sonnet, and like all sonnets this one has been inspired by an extraordinary woman. My own 'dark lady.'" I thought that was a pretty impressive Shakespearean reference to sneak into the introduction. Then I began:

You saw when I stumbled. You saw when I fell.
You didn't care, you said, and helped me up.
You taught me all the secrets you could tell,
your eyes as clear as water in a cup

My heart was just a lamp that gave no light
until you taught me not to be alone.
Your hair as bright as fire in the night,
I hear your voice when I cannot hear my own

Now nothing matters till I know you've heard
the things I say. The electric heat of skin
burns on my fingers when I touch your hand.
I eep on wainting for the perfect words
to say how I feel, to help us begin,
knowing only you can understand.

When I finished, there was thunderous applause from my table of friends, and an "Oh my!" from Maggie, who had turned a serious shade of pink. Scrooge gave me a thumbs-up from the judges' panel. The rest of the audience seemed vaguely appreciative, too, since mine was the only poem so far that seemed the least bit, well . . . poetic.

When I reached the table, I was a deep shade of pink myself. I felt like I'd put an awful lot of myself on display, maybe far too much.

"What schmaltz!" Jeremy cried. "How long did it take you to come up with lines like that?"

The others ignored him. "Awesome," said Allison. "Incredible," said Hannah. The rest of my friends tossed around similar adjectives, but the nicest compliment I received came from poet number one. The older man tapped me on the shoulder, then said, "Wish I could write like that."

Well, how about that, I said to myself.

None of this approval mattered, of course, if the dark lady of my sonnet wasn't impressed. I wasn't sure how she felt. Maggie seemed a little guarded when I sat down, as if she were holding back some big emotion of her own.

But then Maggie grabbed my arm, squeezing it, and whispered in my ear. "Did you mean it?"

"Of course I meant it," I replied. My face got very close to hers.

"Really mean it?" she asked. "I mean, you weren't just making it up to write a pretty sonnet, or were you?"

"No, I meant it," I said. "I didn't just make it up. I've been feeling it, all year. It just took me a long time to understand what I was feeling."

"Oh, Al," she sighed, then nuzzled her face against my shoulder. "I thought it was only me."

Our friends, bless their hearts, looked tactfully away. They pretended to be watching poet number six, or stirring their drinks, or staring into space. It's funny how a little authentic emotion seems to make everyone shy. Even Jeremy, who must have been thinking all sorts of lascivious thoughts, said nothing to break the moment.

The glow lasted all of thirty seconds, until Melissa Halvorsen made her way between the tables and stopped at ours. Her thoughts were succinct: "What a load of crap." Then she pushed on, heading towards the washrooms.

Maggie lifted her head from my arm. "To think, I selected her to start your dating life. What was I thinking?"

"What are you thinking now?" I asked her.

"Later," she whispered. "Later."

The other poets read their works while we sat, drinking more pitchers of beer, applauding anyone who was good, or funny, or really bizarre. Among the good poets was a woman, poet number eight, who delivered an ode in an Irish lilt that made me think of William Butler Yeats. In fact, the poem was so good I wondered if Yeats had actually written it. There was also a male poet who looked like a university professor, but his poem was so full of dense literary language that it was hard to determine what, if anything, it meant.

When all fifteen poets had finished, the judges put their heads together and the announcer went back with a calculator. There were a few tense minutes while the deliberations went on, and then the announcer returned to the stage.

The judges have s-s-select-t-ted f-f-five p-p-poets for the s-s-econd round. They are p-poets numbers f-f-four, f-f-five, eight, eleven, and twelve."

There was another round of applause and some clapping on the back for me. I beamed. My first public performance as a poet and I had made the first cut. *Not bad, Al*, I told myself. *Not bad at all.* With Maggie's head pressed against me, I was feeling very, very good indeed.

"What are you going to read this time?" Maggie asked me.

"Another sonnet," I said.

"How many do you have?"

"About a dozen, but not enough."

"Not enough for what?"

"Not enough to do you justice."

Now that, I decided, was a very smooth line. The only problem with it as a "line" was that it was true.

In the second round, poet four kept on with his body-parts theme, this time offering "Beating Heart," a succession of sounds that would have been a good soundtrack for one of those reality medical shows. Poet five, me, offered one more sonnet about his red-headed beloved, this one not quite as good as the first, but good enough to garner a standing ovation from my group of fans. Poet number eight did another Yeats-like poem about a local lake, a poem full of wonderful sounds and evocative language that deserved far more applause than it received. Poet number eleven did a poem about tattoos, but it was a bit heavy on the needles and a bit weak on the imagery. Then poet number twelve got up, stared at the audience with dark eyes, and delivered a wonderfully musical poem so full of sound and rhythm, that I wasn't sure what it really meant.

There was a surge of applause. Was his poem that good? I don't know. But the performance was terrific and poet number twelve deserved his ovation.

The judges compared their score sheets as we ordered one more pitcher of beer. Maggie was holding onto my arm so tightly I thought she might cut off circulation. I think she was more worried about my making the final round than I was myself.

"F-f-for the f-f-final r-r-round: poets five, eight, and t-t-twelve!"

Maggie turned to me with a wonderful smile. The rest of our

group began thumping their mugs on the table, chanting: "Five, five, five, five!"

I wasn't ready for this. By now, I thought, I'd be eliminated from the competition and cheerfully consoling myself with a few more glasses of beer. But now there was a chance, just a chance, that I might win.

"You can do it, Alan," Maggie whispered.

"Knock 'em dead, Al," added Jeremy.

I was trembling. I had written a dozen sonnets, but not a dozen *good* sonnets. Sonnets are hard to write, I found, even if you don't bother to rhyme the lines. There are all these structural problems, all these issues of form and rhythm that a real poet knows how to handle. I wasn't a real poet. I was an amateur, a beginner.

And I was terrified.

"You'll be fine," Maggie said, kissing me on my cheek. I think she was trying to give me courage.

"You're the man," Scrooge added.

I didn't feel much like the man as I approached the first of three barstools on the stage. I felt like a guy who'd already spent his two best poems and was now reaching into the bottom of a pretty empty satchel hoping for a verse that wasn't there yet.

There were new rules now. The audience's applause and yells of appreciation would be measured on some kind of machine, and the winner determined by volume alone. Scrooge shrieked when that was announced, and I thought, for a moment, that my friends' noise might overcome any deficiency in the poem I was about to read.

"Poet number five, Alan M-m-macklin."

Ah, I had a name now.

"I, uh, well," I began stupidly, "this is not a sonnet. It is a . . . a . . . I'm not sure, really, but here it is."

The audience grew hushed. I began to read.

Listen to the drumbeat
that beats in every single thing.

Listen to the perfect song
I never learned to sing.

Look up at the rings of fire
in every stormy sky
and watch the famous runner
who's always passing by.

The drumbeat is my heart, my love.
The runner is my need.
The fire is my burning,
and the song I couldn't sing

Is about the secret moment
and the waiting and the yearning
and the way two lovers cling
and the song they learn to sing.

I confess, my voice cracked a bit as the last lines came out. Too much feeling always breaks me up a little. But my friends covered for me by going overboard with noise: there was shrieking and whooping and applauding and stomping and pounding of beer mugs on the table. The rest of the audience was polite, but not quite as enthusiastic. Sill, I was a contender based on volume alone.

Poet number eight was actually named Evelyn Turner, a member of the local poetry guild and obviously a considerable fan of Yeats. Her next poem was another perfectly constructed, brilliantly rhymed ode that might have brought down the house in 1912. Unfortunately, the response today was more reserved. Without a band of fanatics to make noise, she was definitely out of the running.

So it was Al Macklin versus poet number twelve, B. J. Stewart.

The poet with the penetrating eyes and rhythmical but incomprehensible verses.

This time, he began with a little prologue. "I want to dedicate this to Gillian," he said, and then he began.

"Ever since ever, since ever since, ever since ever, ever since that day, that day, that . . ."

He looked at the audience.

"That day you left."

We expected a poem full of sound and perhaps fury that would ultimately come to signify nothing at all. Instead we got a beautiful love poem, one that sounded like the very best of e. e. cummings, delivered with reverence and respect and even love.

At its conclusion, the audience was on its feet—even my friends—giving poet number twelve the applause that he and his poem so richly deserved. There was no way that my beginner verses could compete. B.J. Stewart had won the contest for performance, authenticity, and sheer poetry.

I joined in the applause, then left the stage as the announcer came forward with an envelope in his hand. We assumed that this would entitle winning poet number twelve to his dozen free pitchers for the summer that was still to come.

I got back to my table of friends, offering a little shrug and a wan smile. I was about to sit down when Maggie stood up and grabbed me.

"Come on, we're going," she said.

"Where?" I asked.

"My place. You get the runner-up prize."

Then she dragged me out the door.

26

At Last

"SO THIS IS IT?" I said. It was only half a question.

"This is it," Maggie replied.

"How do we start?"

"Kiss me."

We had taken a cab to Maggie's apartment building. Her dad was off fishing with some of his friends from the board of education maintenance department, so we had the place to ourselves. The apartment was dark when we got there, but Maggie put on only one light before she found a bunch of tea candles and some matches. Soon there were a dozen tiny lights glowing in the living room. Then Maggie went off to the kitchen and handed me another beer. "To loosen you up," Maggie said, because I really was nervous. No, terrified would be a better word. At last, this was it.

"A big kiss?" I asked her.

"Any size," she replied. "But don't stop kissing until I say so."

This was no problem. Maggie has always been a wonderful kisser. Maggie knew just how to do it—just how far to open her lips, just how much to play with my tongue, just when to stop for a breath so we could kiss again.

"So was it the poetry? I asked.

"No, it was the feeling behind the poetry."

"That's real," I said.

"I know."

"So you felt it, too?"

"Yeah, me too."

The dialogue of lovers is never profound. Maybe that's why we need poetry to make sense of our feelings, to give words to the intensity. When we're there—touching, kissing, feeling—the words get lost.

"We're both virgins, you know," Maggie said. She had unbuttoned my shirt.

"Well, kind of," I said. I unzipped my pants. Why hadn't I worn sexier underwear?

She shook her head. "What happened to me in Vermont doesn't count. That wasn't making love. It wasn't even real sex." She paused. "Unzip me, please."

Oh, those wonderful words. I think *Unzip me, please* should be in phrase books for foreign travellers, along with *Your place or mine?* and *My goodness, you're so big!* Surely these are the words that any traveller really needs.

"So you're a spiritual virgin, and I'm a physical virgin."

"Yeah, that's it," she said, shrugging so the dress fell down to her feet. "Do you want to take off my bra?"

"Yeah, I'd like that," I said.

I had to wrestle with the little clasps at the back for a bit, but then the bra unhooked and joined Maggie's dress in a pile on a chair. Maggie's breasts were beautiful, more beautiful than I could have imagined.

"The freckles kind of stop," I said, bending down to tease her.

"Mmm, that's good," Maggie said. "Be gentle, now."

"I'm always gentle."

"But not too gentle."

"Like this?"

"Yeah, that's good."

I think the problem with making out is in the contradictions. How much is too much? How fast should a guy go? How do you read the signs, the sighs, the sweet little intakes of breath?

"Okay, we've got to stop for a second."

We pulled back from each other. My pants were now bundled around my ankles, my socks were still on my feet, and my underwear had formed a tent. I probably looked ridiculous.

Maggie, on the other hand, looked wonderful.

"A thong?" I asked.

"Just for you."

"Really?"

Maggie said nothing, then pulled it off. She was nude. Now I had to scramble to get out of the rest of my clothes.

"You're beautiful," I said.

"No, I'm not," she replied. "But thank you for the thought."

"So that was it?" I said.

"That was it," Maggie replied.

What could I say then? Once again I needed poetry and couldn't come up with even one line. I lay there in silence. No longer a virgin. I sighed and rolled over to kiss Maggie again.

"Was it good?"

"Wonderful. And for you."

"Very nice," she sighed. "Now I have a hunch you want to do it again."

"Well, yeah. But that was my only condom. What do we do?"

"We get one from the bathroom, dummy," she told me. "No way I'm going to end up pregnant like your mother."

27

Poet Laureate

I THINK THE MORNING-AFTER glow from sex can be better than sex itself . . . or almost as good. There is something quite wonderful—no *exquisite,* that's the word—about lying in bed while your lover runs off to the kitchen and returns with coffee and croissants.

"I love you," I said, as Maggie handed me a coffee mug.

"You're blathering," she replied. "This morning, you *think* you love me, but tomorrow, we'll see." She put the plate on the bedspread. "Now be careful with the croissant; I don't want crumbs all over my bed." Then she kissed me.

I sipped my coffee. "Do you want to know when I figured out I was in love with you?

"When?" Maggie asked. She snuggled up against me.

"When you called me a dolt," I said. "Remember in that email? Actually, I think you said I was a delightful dolt."

"And that made you love me?"

"No, that's when I realized that I already loved you. Because I wasn't mad when you wrote that. I wasn't hurt, even though it was true. I just went, like, this girl knows who I really am and she still likes me, and then there was this kind of shiver that went up my spine."

Maggie kissed me. It was a big kiss, flavoured with coffee and croissants. "I more than liked you, you dolt. I fell for you last year. I probably fell for you two years ago."

"You did?"

"But I couldn't tell you. We were going to school on opposite sides of the country. And I was afraid I'd get hurt. I mean, you spent your first year at college trying desperately to get laid with every girl under the sun, and I was just waiting. That's all I could do. But every time you emailed me about some girl, I'd be seething."

"Sorry, I didn't know."

"I knew you didn't know. That trollop in Puerto Vallarta had to be the low point."

"Yeah, she was. Maybe that's when I figured it out."

"Figured what out?"

"That I love you," I said, kissing her—a little kiss.

"You do?"

"I love that you can use the word *trollop* in a sentence, when I have to guess what it means. I love that you're so smart, and so beautiful, and so patient . . . and so ticklish."

"Stop, I'll spill my coffee."

"I'll stop if we could do something else," I said.

"Again?" she asked.

"If you'd be so kind."

For a man who, just a few months previously, had been suffering from erectile dysfunction, I must say that I impressed myself. I just needed the right woman for everything to work exactly as it should. Ah, the relief.

Later that morning, I called my parents to say that I'd be staying with a friend for the weekend. They didn't bother to ask questions. They were so hung up on having a mid-life baby that I'd been deleted from their desktop.

Maggie, of course, loved the irony of my mom's pregnancy, especially after all the "be careful" lectures from my father. It became one of our shared giggles.

A little later, Scrooge called and Maggie handed me the phone.

"Hey, Al, my man," Scrooge began, as he does.

"How'd you know I'd be here at Maggie's?"

"Never underestimate my genius," Scrooge told me. "All the rest of us could see it coming, we just wondered what took you so long."

I was beginning to wonder that myself.

"Anyhow," he went on, "I just called to tell you that you got the runner-up prize, or maybe I should say that *we* got the runner-up prize. Drank it all last night, since you two had other plans."

"Yeah, great."

"I'm thinking of writing some poetry myself," Scrooge said. "Seems to have a kind of sex appeal for a certain kind of woman, you know, the brainy ones."

"Seems funny that you'd be learning moves from me," I said.

"As the great Bart Simpson once said, you're never too old to learn. You two have a good time today, you probably deserve it. Took you long enough."

Maggie asked me about lunch, and for a minute I thought she might actually make something for us. In fact, she was waiting for me to put together a couple of sandwiches; Maggie's culinary skills were limited to coffee and croissants.

I opened a bottle of wine, too, just to celebrate our first twelve hours as lovers. By the time we'd finished it, we'd been lovers for fourteen hours and I was a bit giddy from the wine.

"Do you think Kirk would marry us?" I asked her.

"I think Kirk should get ordained first," Maggie said. "And maybe we should both graduate, and then maybe you should ask me nicely."

"I thought I just did," I said.

"No, you have to get down on your knees and have the ring in your hands. Then there's got to be some gushy prologue, and wild protestations of love, and the famous words 'Will you marry me?'"

"You're still giving me advice, Maggie," I sighed.

She smiled and kissed me. "Hey, keep it up and I might keep giving you advice for a long, long time."

Acknowledgements

THE AUTHOR GIVES HIS THANKS to many people who helped in this second Alan novel: to my friend, the distinguished poet David Helwig, who pinch-wrote two poems for Alan in Chapter 25 and then let me meddle with them; to my assistant, Kenda Berg, who reported on her Cancun holiday to help with the Puerto Vallarta section; to my editor at Doubleday, Amy Black, who gave me lots of leeway but managed to keep this book within the young-adult genre; and to my wife and muse, Lori Jamison, who reads every word several times over with loving attention.

About the Author

PAUL KROPP is the author of more than fifty novels for young people. His work includes seven award-winning young adult novels, many books for reluctant readers, and four illustrated books for beginning readers. He also writes non-fiction books and articles for parents, and is a popular speaker on issues related to reading and education.